# Murder on the Night Shift

**Kathy Cohen**

Dedicated to dog lovers everywhere

# CHAPTER ONE

Dusk was just settling in, only a few lights shining down the face of the Westshore Lake Apartments as Sue Anne approached from the west. It was hot and humid, but the girl, speeding through the upper class neighborhood in her dark blue Mercedes, didn't notice. She was irritated about something.

Construction in the area was far from complete. Trees were establishing roots still, homes were going up here and there yet, and sod trucks rolled in and out often. Everything had the nice, shiny stamp of newness about it mainly because an elderly farmer had refused to sell the land, forcing local developers to wait until he died (fairly recently) to get their hands on it. But the apartment building, one of the first structures undertaken, had been there for several years.

Not that long ago Sue Anne would have paused to admire the twelve story building's reflection in the lake developers had dredged east of it; she would also have swelled with pride at the liveried doorman waiting behind the glass doors of the lobby to assist its wealthy renters. The youngest of eight, used to hand-me-downs and discards, she'd been open-mouthed when Howie'd taken her on a tour, given her a glimpse of the luxurious surroundings. Compared to the tiny one-bedroom dump she shared with her girlfriend Shirley, it was a palace. "When do I move in?" she'd asked Howie.

Shirley had disapproved and tried to talk her out of it. "What do you want to hook up with somebody like Howard Margolin for? Christ, he's old enough to be your father. Not to mention all the people who live there are old. How the hell you figure you'll fit in?" She'd been jealous, that was all, strung out on all those drugs and looking thirty-five if she looked a day.

She'd moved in the following week, letting Howie buy new furnishings for the place, generously allowing Shirley to keep the communal junk. It hadn't taken a week to accustom herself to the blue-tinted hair and the lap dogs, the Phoenix tans and the disapproving frowns. What did she care? Twenty-five years old with nothing but a high school diploma, a great figure and fingers that could type eighty words a minute only after snorting some coke, she knew a good thing when she saw it. Or thought she did. Now, however, she squealed down the ramp to the basement garage taking her surroundings in stride. Almost two years of luxurious living had spoiled her. She was mad. If there was anything that got her riled, it was having her time wasted. Not to mention the fact that she might have missed a phone call.

She rode the elevator to the tenth floor, let herself in the end unit, and poured herself a scotch. Clunking a few ice cubes into her glass, she strode through the living room and down the hall to the bedroom. Clothes lay everywhere, and she flopped down on the king-sized bed with a sigh. Saturday night and here she was, lying on her butt. Somebody'd said they'd come by later, but who could count on that? Who cared, anyway? She sighed, rolled over and pulled a tray of stash out from under her bed. Poking through the pharmacy of vials, she found the Vicodin, swallowed two with the Scotch, then opened a baggie of marijuana. With practiced fingers she rolled a joint, held it over a gold lighter until it was dry, then lit it, drawing the air deep into her lungs.

Poor Shirl, she thought as the image of her ex-room-mate came to mind. What would ever come of her drifting from job to job, hanging out with those sleazeballs she called friends? It was the drugs that did it. Shirley had never been able to control them, use them only now and again like she did. You had to know your limit, be able to back away when you suspected a dependency developing, she'd told Shirley time and time again.

The last time Shirley had been by she'd been surprised, no shocked at her friend's appearance. "You trying to kill yourself?" she'd asked. Shirley'd only grinned, told her to hurry, her friend was waiting in the car. God only knew what he looked like, she thought. Some bum from skid row no doubt. No, she was lucky, if you looked at it the way she did. She'd ignored Shirley's advice and gotten herself quite a deal by hooking up with Howie. The apartment, the car, the jewelry . . .

Which wasn't about to end, she told herself confidently as she thought of the scene the night before: Howie yelling at her, his face contorted, the veins on his neck standing out; her yelling back, throwing things. He'd come around, she pacified herself. He always did. It was the other one doing it, she thought as she began to feel the affects of the drugs and alcohol. It hadn't been a bright idea getting involved with him, she thought, staring dreamily at the ceiling as a rush passed through her. He was a nice guy and all, but there were too many problems, too much emotional baggage weighing him down. She could see him in her mind's eye loping though a field in waning light, his expression solemn, his eyes focused into the distance. And then another rush hit her. Wow, this was good stuff.

When she tried to picture him again she couldn't. Now she was the one riding through the decreasing light, the churning power between her legs urgent, the landscape a confused kaleidoscope of fertile green. Her eyes closed. After a while she lost consciousness.

Ellie Schimmel tapped a couple of keys and watched figures stride rapidly backwards, climb into a car with inverted motions, and zoom off, headlights disappearing into the warm darkness. That scene segued into one of a full-faced man with a goatee and sideburns, his face alternately serious then wistful, serious then amused, who melted into a black-tie crowd. Finally, a crystal chandelier appeared, suspended from the ceiling of the elaborate Orpheum lobby. Mayor O'Hanley, viewed in reverse at a fundraiser for the local zoo. Too boring for words.

Ellie sighed, saved the file, and switched out the lights in the editing room. Television news was nothing like she'd imagined it back in college, where assigned reading like "Investigative Reporting: Morals, Methods and the Public," and lectures about Woodward and Bernstein's historic work made her anxious to matriculate, get out into the real world where she could put her fledgling reportorial skills to the test. She trudged down the hall to the newsroom. Her Reeboks made a squeaking sound on the linoleum.

Ellie sat down at an empty desk and closed her eyes. Domestic disturbances and personal injury accidents were what it all boiled down to when you were new, got stuck on the night shift, and had no contacts. She consulted her watch and groaned. Three a.m. was too far away. She had almost nodded off when a faint squawk from the police radio brought her back to life. A domestic disturbance perhaps? She listened attentively for several minutes, then slumped back in her chair. Apparently not. God, things had never been slower; she was really bored if she was disappointed about that. A little later one of the engineers, Ray, she thought his name was, poked his head in the newsroom door. "Looks like you're busy tonight."

"The stress is killing me."

"Want a soda? I'm going down for one."

"Sure. The caffeine might keep me awake."

He disappeared.

Everyone had deserted her shortly after eleven like they always did. The news ended and off they trooped, anxious to go home to their families or to meet friends at clubs and local bars. She, on the other hand, was expected to stick around in case "something popped." That's how News Director Fred Burrows had put it during the employment interview where she'd crossed the line from intern to full-time hire.

"The other stations don't have anyone sticking around much past midnight," he'd said, "and I think it's worth a try. Willing to handle it alone?"

Of course, she'd said. She had not only studied to be a broadcast journalist, but she'd tacked on classes in photography and videotape editing to make herself more employable. She knew that was why she'd been hired and Burrows would consider having her there alone late at night. She was a one-man band. Not only could she cover and write the story, but she could shoot and edit it as well.

When Ray came back with her soda, she made him sit down and keep her company. He didn't mind, she told herself. What did he have to do that late at night?

A buzzing noise broke the silence. Sue Anne swam through several layers of unconsciousness, struggling to open her eyes. What was it? Had she heard something? She waited, comfortable and warm, had begun the gradual decline back to oblivion when the buzzing started again. The doorbell. That's what it was. She opened her eyes, finally managed to sit up.

The room reeled. When it stopped, her eyes lit on the

tray of drugs on the floor. She cast around for a place to hide it, just in case. First she shoved it under her bed, decided that wasn't safe, stuffed it in a drawer, thought that wasn't safe either, then forgot about it when she caught a glimpse of herself in the dressing table mirror. The whites of her eyes almost matched the red of her silk blouse. She giggled. It was hard even lifting her eyelids to see that much.

She swiped at the bright-blond halo of hair that almost reached her shoulders, grinned at the hazy reflection that stared good-humoredly back at her, then wondered what it would be like to have an identical twin. I'd still be prettier, she thought smugly. People would compare us and say, "Sue Anne's the thinner one with the big boobs and the great face. The one who deserves the furs and the cars and the trips."

The doorbell buzzed again, and she stumbled down the hall to the dimly-lit living room. "All right, already, keep your shirt on," she mumbled. The room began to revolve slowly as she entered it, the long, low couch stretching even longer, lower, as it spun. She grabbed at the wall to steady herself. When it stopped, her eyes lit on the stereo, bathed in moonlight, and as she passed by she switched it on. Katy Perry's newest erupted from the speakers. Why the hell are the sliding glass doors open with the air on, she wondered as a slight breeze off the balcony wafted the sheers into clouds. Clouds like the ones in my brain, she giggled. She heard what sounded, over Katy, like faraway knocking.

"I told you I was coming," she said, remembering in a rush why she had gotten up, stumbled out to the front room. After a struggle, she got the door open, frowned. Her brain shifted gears, speeding up slightly. "That's right. You said you were coming by."

Her visitor, for some reason, seemed displeased, stepped past her with a curt nod. "Under the weather?"

She nodded, closed the door, tried to phrase a question

that made sense. "Why?" But her tongue felt thick, didn't seem to want to work and she fell silent, turned around to see her visitor disappearing down the hall toward the bedroom. A wave of nausea closed over her, and she put a shaky hand to her forehead, sank down on the couch. "I feel kinda sick," she said, but with competition over the airways from Katy Perry, this went unheard. She needed a glass of water maybe, or some juice to settle her stomach. She'd ask her guest to get it for her.

But when she sensed the returned presence, she had already forgotten what it was she wanted, could complain only that she was sick again.

"Why don't you lie down," it was suggested and she complied, turning over on her stomach, closing her eyes. Soon the nausea subsided, replaced by a pleasant sort of paralysis. Her visitor said something, paused as if waiting for a reply, began to speak again, this time close to her ear, but she couldn't comprehend the words, noticed only the droning quality so unlike the rock music blaring from the stereo. She stretched out, cradled one cheek with her arm. Soon she'd forgotten her visitor. As she began to doze, she saw rivers of glass falling gently in cascading ribbons, pooling in frothy circles far below, while birds reeled and circled in the blue expanse overhead. They called mournfully to one another. Finally she slept. The diamond, set in the long-ruby-colored nail of her index finger, twinkled. Her visitor didn't stay long.

# CHAPTER TWO

Margaret Simpson woke up and looked around her bedroom as though she were on an alien planet. Finally she oriented herself. Yes, that was her lamp, her afghan, her pillow. With advancing age she'd been having trouble falling asleep at night, but certainly no trouble waking up suddenly. She looked at the luminous dial of her alarm clock. 12:50. She'd tramped up and down all twelve flights today (only eight yesterday—could that be the problem?) and she ought to be tired. Why'd anybody ever invent elevators anyway, she wondered fitfully. Might be more healthy tickers like hers if people didn't rely on all the modern conveniences so much.

Maybe it was that blasted music across the hall. Rock music, wasn't that what they called it? Margaret wrapped the afghan around her shoulders and went out to the living room where the noise was even more deafening. That girl across the hall was always playing her music, but she didn't think it had ever been this late. I'll just march across the hall and tell her to turn it off, Margaret decided. She dropped the afghan, donning her raincoat instead, and opened the door.

Mr. Olson from 908 downstairs was walking hesitantly down the brightly lit hallway, scuffing his slippers in the royal blue carpet. "Can't sleep," he called when he spotted Margaret. She was tempted to spirit the eligible old widower into her apartment for a cup of hot tea (with some sherry perhaps?) and let the young girl continue her party, but she didn't see how she could explain herself going out so late at night in a raincoat no less, so she redoubled her indignation and the two of them rang the girl's doorbell. After doing that several times, they resorted to knocking and then pounding. After a few minutes, they agreed it was time to get the manager.

Ten minutes later, a shaken Mr. Holling was calling 911. Margaret got her wish. Mr. Olson thought a little sherry would be nice under the circumstances.

The engine on her Volkswagen roared as Ellie wheeled into the parking lot next to the high-rise. A police car partially blocked the entrance, but she saw no sign of other reporters. Shouldering the video camera and a set of lights, she hurried up the walk and nodded brusquely to the doorman, who pointed to the elevators. So far so good. But the police wouldn't be so gullible. On the tenth floor, still no patrolmen in sight, she doubled her pace. If she could just get inside, get some footage before they muscled her out.

"There's a dead body in there," an elderly woman standing outside the apartment she sought said as she approached. "It's my neighbor."

Ellie nodded, rounded the turn, then stopped short. She was inside, she'd made it in, and there still weren't any cops. What the hell was going on? She took in the plum colored carpeting, the modern furniture, the walkout balcony in a glance, noted that there were no signs of a disturbance. The room appeared empty. And then her eyes focused on the body in front of her, obscured at first by the high-backed couch on which it lay. Ellie stepped forward hesitantly, puzzled.

It was a woman, stretched out full-length in front of her, face down. Whoever she was, she looked comfortable, as if she were asleep. Her face was hidden by a profusion of blond hair, but, by the style of her clothing, the whiff of expensive-smelling perfume hovering over her, Ellie judged her to be between twenty and forty. That she was dead was obvious, Ellie'd seen enough accident victims to know. But how? And why?

Ellie stepped closer. There was no blood, no obvious wound she could see, but, as she leaned over to study the stone set in the nail of one of the woman's dagger-like nails—a diamond?—a livid bruise on the back of the dead woman's neck suddenly became visible to her through the bright hair.

"Who are you? Press?"

Ellie spun around, took an involuntary step away from the body, almost bumped into the patrolman staring questioningly at her. "Yes, WBTV Officer . . ." she looked for his name tag, "McDaniels."

"You didn't touch anything did you?"

"Of course not." Ellie quelled her indignation. Where in hell had he come from? He looked young, was staring at her expectantly. A rookie, she decided. He didn't have his procedures down pat yet. She put down the video camera and lights and pulled out her notebook. "What happened here, Officer?"

"Could be a homicide," McDaniels said.

Ellie felt her pulse quicken. She kept her expression bland. "Was she strangled, do you think?"

"You saw the bruises, eh?" He shook his head ruefully. "Well now, that's for the Medical Examiner to say for sure."

Ellie threw out questions as fast as she could think of them, knowing their interview couldn't last long. Was anything missing? Were there signs of forced entry? Had neighbors heard anything, seen anything? Had he found evidence of drugs?

To all of them he shook his head, said he didn't know yet;

but on the last, she thought she saw a flicker of something. He'd seen something back in the bedroom. That must have been where he'd come from.

"What about a name? Do you have a name yet?"

"Yes. But we have to make sure it's her. And notify next-of-kin. Sorry." He smiled regretfully.

"How old do you think she is?"

"Mid-twenties."

Mid-twenties. That meant the victim was about her age. "Who found the body?"

Now it was McDaniel's turn to consult his notes. "A Mr. Holling. Manager of the building. Had complaints from across the hall of loud music, knocked, let himself in when nobody answered the door. My partner and I heard about it on the radio and came over. Speak of the devil. Another uniformed patrolman stood at the front door looking quizzically from Ellie to Officer McDaniels.

"Who's this?"

"Miss . . ." McDaniels looked at Ellie.

"Schimmel," Ellie said smoothly. "From WBTV."

The patrolman met her smile with a scowl. "I just left the rest of the press in the lobby with instructions to stay there. How'd you get up here, and what do you think you're doing?"

Ellie scooped up her paraphernalia and backed out while McDaniels and his partner exchanged words about securing a crime scene. The elderly couple was gone, she saw, the door to 1007 firmly closed. She thought briefly about knocking, thought better of it when two plainclothes detectives got out of the elevator and headed in her direction. One of them, a dark-haired, swarthy man she got the impression might be in charge, nodded as they passed, giving her a thin lipped smile. Who was he, she wondered as the elevator returned her soundlessly to the lobby.

And then she forgot about him, had no time for further conjecture, as she was pounced on by the two newspapermen waiting in the lobby. How had she gotten up there, one of them wondered suspiciously, while the other one told him not to worry about that, the important thing was to find out what she now knew. At least they weren't television reporters, she consoled herself as she began to fill them in. Fred Burrows would be happy. Out of the corner of her eye, she noticed that the doorman who had sent her upstairs in the first place was eyeing them curiously. Stout, in his sixties, his doorman's hat slightly off center, he was edging toward them, no doubt in hopes of doing a little eavesdropping.

"Anybody question him?" Ellie interrupted the older reporter in mid-sentence.

"He gave us a name," the younger one she thought worked for the *Sentinel* said, flipping rapidly through his notes. "And a boyfriend's. Let's see. If the victim is the woman who lives in that apartment, her name is Sue Anne Cavanaugh. And that would make the boyfriend someone named Howard Margolin. Molina, that's the doorman, says Margolin is about his age and the woman's considerably younger."

Ellie wrinkled her forehead. Hadn't she heard one of those names before? "You see the Cavanaugh woman or Howard Margolin tonight?" she asked Molina suddenly, turning to face him.

"Never saw him," the doorman said, not at all surprised at his sudden inclusion in the conversation, "but I saw her around eight or so pulling into the underground parking in her Mercedes. Driving like a bat out of hell like she usually did."

"Is there another entrance to the building down there?"

"Sure there is. Little lobby with an elevator."

"What's the security like?"

He scratched his jaw. "Well, there's nobody down there

patrolling, if that's what you mean. But it's well-lit, and no-body can enter the elevator without a tenant's key. There's never been any trouble. . ."

"See anybody come in through here who looked suspicious tonight?"

He shook his head. "And I've been here since six. Except during my break around nine that is when I propped the front doors open and went downstairs to get me a cup of coffee."

Ellie asked the next obvious question. "You do this every night? Prop the doors open during your break?"

He nodded, grinned. "Except when it's raining or snowing. Then my wife sends me off with a thermos, and I stay put. I don't think management would like it if I let rain or snow in."

There you had it. If the crime was premeditated, the entry time was nine o'clock sharp, Ellie thought. The perpetrator could have waltzed in naked, wheeled in a cannon, led in a roaring lion and this guy wouldn't know about it. "Can you tell me anything about the couple's relationship?" she asked him. "Did you talk with them much?"

Ed shook his head, looking surprised. Only the older folks chatted with him, he said, and then only a select few. Most of the tenants ignored him. The building housed very wealthy people, he said matter-of-factly, not the kind of folks who cared to have conversations with him. Margolin had come by once or twice a week maybe for the last couple of years, but he doubted they'd exchanged a dozen words. "He did have me call a cab once to take him and her to the airport." As for her, she came and went daily, mostly via the parking garage. But she never spoke.

Ellie turned to look as the crime lab vehicle guys rapped on the door and Ed straightened his hat, strode importantly towards them.

Mr. Holling, the manager, wasn't so friendly. Clearly resenting their presence, he waved the three of them off irritably when he emerged from the elevators, barking a hoarse "no comment," and slamming the door to his office behind him. But Ellie made do with videotape, and she was pleased watching the finished product on the monitor in the newsroom six odd hours later. The visual story told it all.

She'd begun with a long-shot of the apartment building, dark except for the lobby and a few windows on upper floors. Then an ambulance pulling up to the entrance into her shot, lights flashing. Next a close-up of the ambulance attendants wheeling out the body, a cutaway of two uniformed cops (McDaniels and the unfriendly one) talking to the manager, a few frames of the attendants loading the body and then a head-shot of the detective, Bieterman, making his statement. One of the newspapermen said he'd met him before, the cop had been around. He hadn't proven very talkative. Ellie's accompanying narrative had lasted all of thirty seconds. The monitor went dark, and Ellie lobbed her styrofoam coffee cup in the waste basket. "Thanks," she told the video editor, who nodded wordlessly.

Fred Burrows, she could see through the glass partitions that separated his office from the newsroom, was on the phone. Talking about her, she decided, when she overheard him saying something about being there when it counted, and then more about patience usually paying off. Perfect timing to make her pitch, she decided, settling into a chair across the desk from him, waiting for his conversation to end.

"I just heard we're the only station with video this morning," he said, slamming down the phone suddenly. "Nice going."

Ellie smiled. "What say you keep me on the story since I did such a good job? I'll come in on my own time and continue working my shift, too. You could pair me with Mitch, and I could get some valuable experience." It was impossible to gauge his reaction. He ran his hand through his gray-flecked crewcut, adjusted his bow tie, said nothing.

"I need some stimulation," she continued, trying not to spread it on too thick, but not wanting the argument too minimal to let him know she cared. "Nothing ever happens at night. I'm stagnating. Personal injury accidents and domestic disturbances have gotten old."

"So last night was a cakewalk?"

Ellie grinned. "The point is I've been working that shift for six months, and this is the first newsworthy event I've covered. Doesn't it make sense to let me follow it through to the end?"

The news manager pulled foil off a stick of gum and stuck it in his mouth while he considered. As an afterthought he offered her a piece. She declined.

"I don't mean to sound ungrateful," she started, then dropped that. Burrows wasn't the kind to be buttered up by thanks for her employment. She'd already done that when he'd hired her, and once was enough. "This won't cost you a dime," she said instead. "I wouldn't dream of putting in for overtime. Think of it as free on-the-job-training."

"When would you sleep?"

"That's my problem. I'm young. I don't need much."

"What about Mitch?" That was a thornier issue. Both of them knew Mitch Bassman, the police beat reporter, wouldn't consider it an honor to have a rookie following him around.

"You'll talk to him. Tell him I'll stay out of his way."

Burrows frowned, shuffled through some papers on his desk. While he made his decision, Ellie looked out at the newsroom. No one was around but Bassman, on the phone in a front cubicle, an indolent expression on his broad face.

While she didn't know the man herself—he worked days while she worked nights—she'd heard enough muttering to know he wasn't popular at the station. He was a know-it-all, self-centered, take-charge-type who wouldn't listen to anybody else. That he was married was considered one of the modern mysteries of all times. His wife, so it went, was a doormat, constantly fetching and toting for him; one of the reporters had joked that somebody'd forgotten to clue her in to the change in centuries.

"Send me Bassman, I'll talk to him," Burrows barked suddenly. "But," he admonished as a grin broke out on her face, "I'm going to be watching you. First time you slack off on your regular shift, the deal's off. And get along with Bassman."

No easy task, she told herself soberly, as she marched out to relay the news to the police beat reporter. But she'd have to try. If Burrows pulled her off the story midway because she couldn't be a team player, she might as well hang it up. Cases like this didn't come along very often. And she sure wasn't in the position to get them when they did.

# CHAPTER THREE

Jerry Norgaard had been up since five a.m. feeding, watering and working horses, and his shirt was soaked with sweat. Dismounting a young stud he'd just schooled, he led it into the shady confines of the barn. When his eyes had adjusted to the darkness, he called to his right-hand man emerging from a stall further down the aisle. "Take a break, would you L'Heureux? Clean up Pecos for me?"

Dutifully, the younger man parked his wheelbarrow of manure and took the animal while Norgaard pondered his next mount. The filly, he decided. The new one he thought would prove spooky. In his private tack room he reached for a particular training snaffle and stopped short. It wasn't there. Though gleaming bits hung three and four deep on pegs lining the walls, and his students couldn't believe he really knew where every bit hung, the truth was he did. And it was gone.

"I haven't seen it. Bart probably took it," L'Heureux said, hosing lather off the young stud in the shower room.

Shit. He'd told him and told him to ask. Norgaard watched absently as Rich continued his task. With deft, long strokes he scraped the excess water off the horse, starting at the neck and working backwards. Puddles of lather, water, and hair meandered toward the floor drain. "Go ask him," Rich urged. "He's snoring in the lounge." But for some reason he didn't. After a while he went back to the tack room, trying to convince himself an alternate bit would work. Damn that Bart. He saddled the young roan filly, slipped the other bit into her mouth, and led her out to the ring.

Sure enough, she was a timid one, spooked at her own shadow; after she jumped twice while he was leading her, he made an effort to clear his head of distractions, concentrate on what he was doing. He mounted, checked the cinch. Man and horse circled the ring cautiously, the filly tense, her nostrils blowing in and out noisily, the man hunched over, anticipating. This was the first time she'd had a bit in her mouth, and he could hear her working it with her tongue. After two uneventful circles around the ring he relaxed a little, sat up a little straighter in the saddle. She chose that moment to shy violently. Quickly he gathered up the reins and spoke quietly to her until she calmed down. The source of her fright, he saw, was a girl and her horse emerging from a copse of trees at the edge of the field.

Jerry squinted. It was Quinn on her bay gelding. He hadn't known the thirteen-year-old was out, hadn't heard the car door when her father dropped her off at the stable for the day. When she got closer he scowled at her.

"Jerry got a problem?" she asked Rich, sucking on a bottle of soda while she watched him pitch manure in his wheelbarrow a short time later.

"Not that I know of. Why?"

"Seems like kind of a sourpuss."

"He gets that way on a new horse," Rich said. "Don't worry about it."

Don't worry about it. That was all anyone ever said around there. Quinn sniffed contemptuously and went off in search of Bart. She found him where he usually was, in the lounge watching cartoons.

"What's up little lady?" he drawled. Unshaven, dirty, his

24

yellowed socks smelling sour, he was what her father called slothful, a degenerate. Quinn liked him.

"Not much." She sat down, and the pair watched the screen for a while; the girl scornfully, the middle-aged man with evident enjoyment. During a commercial, he swung into a sitting position and pulled on his cowboy boots. He had customers coming, and he guessed he'd better be getting himself presentable he told the girl.

"Think I oughta shave?"

Quinn nodded solemnly.

The commercial ended and so, apparently, did ambition to clean up; he slumped back and smiled as the androgynous little man who hosted the program clapped his hands and exhorted the audience to do the same. Quinn wondered who Bart's clients were and how much they would pay him. "Somebody's going to get killed one of these days," Rich had said darkly, "and then shit's gonna hit the fan." That no one had yet Quinn considered a miracle. She looked sideways at Bart. His eyes were bleary and he looked tired. Drinking again; she'd heard L'Heureux say the man could really put them away. "What did you do last night, Bart?"

But it was the part of the program where the little emcee talked to his imaginary friend, and Bart wanted to hear every word. "Later," he shushed her. Quinn cast a glance around the room, thought about straightening it up a little. Shelves filled with trophies and plaques, belt buckles and trays, lined three walls; the fourth displayed photographs and ribbons. Dust had not discriminated; a thick layer covered everything, and she wondered how Bart could bear to sleep in here. She, herself, endured weekly shots for a variety of allergies, among them mold and dust; her doctor had even suggested she stay away from horses, but of course there was no chance of that.

Where would one even find a cloth? She wrinkled her nose. Jerry may be a one-in-a-million horse trainer, but his attention to daily upkeep was negligible. In the four years she'd known him, taken lessons, hung around the barn, she'd never seen him clean the bathroom, dust the lounge, even straighten his office. His wife, Barbara, told her once she'd decided that with the house and her garden to tend to, she didn't consider it her responsibility. "Besides, I did it all for years with never a thank you, and I figure if he can't be bothered, neither can I."

It didn't hurt his business; all forty stalls were filled, and there was a waiting list of customers he could draw from when anyone left, which was seldom; but still, Quinn wished somebody would do it.

The show ended and Bart switched off the set. "So toots, what's what?" he said absently. She watched him search through a cardboard box in the corner, pull out a rusty straight-edge, some lather, and a towel she wouldn't use to clean up spilled oil on a garage floor, and back through the screen door telling her he'd be back in a flash.

Dust rose when she flopped on the couch he had just vacated, and she was careful to avoid the pillow cover with the faint indentation of his head. Bart was a trip, there were no two ways about that.

L'Heureux, rounding the corner, caught Bart just as he rested his hand on the bathroom doorknob. "You borrow a bit from Jerry?"

Bart turned, grinned. "When?"

"This morning, last night . . . I don't know. Lately."

"Nope. I ain't been on a horse since Thursday."

"Well, did you borrow it then?"

"When?"

"Last Thursday."

"I don't think so, but I'll check my stuff." Bart went into the bathroom and shut the door. God, that guy drove him crazy. What was he, some sort of self-appointed, whatchamacallit, vigilante? He shook his head, turned on the rusty tap, surveyed the thick growth, shook his head again. Women found his hairy body sexy; he found it a pain.

He took it, already sold it, Rich thought as he grasped the handles of the wheelbarrow and maneuvered it around the corner into the sunlight. Son-of-a-bitch. Norgaard was leading the little filly toward him with a preoccupied air, and he hurried to relieve him, listening as the trainer described his ride.

"She's a funny one. Spooky, just like her mother. Hope those people don't put that little girl on her for a few years." The filly looked at them expectantly as if she knew the conversation concerned her, and L'Heureux combed her dark forelock with his fingers, holding her tightly checked in case she jumped. He knew Jerry anguished over mounts like her, warned his clients when he ran across spooky ones, told them not to put inexperienced youngsters on board, and he hastened now to change the subject. "Put me on tomorrow?" he asked earnestly.

Norgaard shook his head. Rich hadn't shown great aptitude as a trainer, and there was no way he'd subject him to such danger. "Not on her, son, but maybe the stud if there's time," he said when he caught L'Heureux's look of disappointment.

He really didn't give him half a chance; nobody learned if they didn't get the opportunity to try.

"Tomorrow," he called more firmly over his shoulder at the retreating figure. "I'll make time tomorrow."

Quinn was sitting by the soda pop machine petting the orange cat, and he smiled at her absently, failing to notice the resultant grin, the relief on the young face. So he wasn't mad at her anymore. Thank goodness. She leaned back on the rough bench and let the cat rub against her, its purring more

27

of a vibration than a noise with the music from the radio so close. She closed her eyes and grinned. Jerry hated the music she and Rich liked, were always turning up when he wasn't around. That was his one flaw. Country western music, love ballads, twangy tunes, how could he call that music? The cat rolled over on her back, pummeled Quinn's hip with her strong back legs while the young girl stroked her stomach. Two younger cats, a calico and a black, chased one another up the ladder to the hayloft, hissing, then disappeared. The music stopped and a couple of commercials followed. Quinn laid her head on the old cat's side, could feel the gentle up-and-down motion as the cat breathed. She was allergic to animal hair, too, and knew she was crazy to be playing with Samantha, but she loved cats and much as she'd always wanted one, had never been able to have one.

"Westshore Lake Apartments was the scene of a homicide early today," a voice on the radio announced after a commercial about whiter teeth, a brighter smile ended. "Police say Sue Anne Cavanaugh, 25, a resident of the plush apartment building, was strangled sometime around midnight last night."

Quinn sat up, feeling for the bench to right herself. Could this be?

"There are few leads at this time. Police, responding to a call from apartment manager Jack Holling, arrived at the scene . . ."

Quinn's mouth had suddenly gone dry. She licked her lips with a tongue that felt too big for her mouth, then stood uncertainly. "Jerry," she called. A water bucket jangled, there was the sound of a hoof stomping on the ground, but otherwise silence. "Jerry," she called more loudly. She trotted a few steps and then started to run. "Jerry, you're not going to believe this . . . "

# CHAPTER FOUR

The view was colorful: upper middle class homes set on rectangular plots of grass, a sparkling blue lake to the east, ribbons of road that faded into prairie grass on the horizon. A toy-like red car pulled into the parking lot and stopped between two white lines. Miniature people got out, slamming the doors.

Ellie let the curtain drop back into place and accepted the cup of tea Margaret Simpson held out to her, watched as the older woman put two teaspoons of sugar in her own and blew on it. She looked exhausted, dark circles marring an otherwise sweet, elderly face. "Imagine a murder taking place across the hall. And that poor girl." Tears came to her eyes and she dabbed at them under her bifocals. "What is the world coming to?"

They were in her kitchen seated at a small table, and Ellie was having flashbacks of visits to her grandmother in Cleveland: handmade potholders on the refrigerator, waxed fruit in a bowl on the counter, plastic doilies under the toaster and the tea kettle.

"You were telling me about discovering the body?"

"That's right." The old woman pursed her lips and in hushed tones resumed her narrative. "I'd been asleep," she said, "when loud music across the hall woke me up. At least

I think it was the loud music that woke me. Who knows? Maybe it was something I ate. Anyway . . . " She told how she and Mr. Olson had awakened the manager, Mr. Holling, after their efforts to get the girl's attention had met with no results. This had been around 12:45 she estimated. Mr. Holling had been annoyed with them for waking him up, but he'd pulled out his master key and opened the door after pounding a couple of times and . . . She paused, pulled a handkerchief out of her pocket, dabbed at her eyes. "We thought she was sleeping. Such a pretty thing she was. The policemen got unnecessarily cross with Mr. Holling as far as I'm concerned, saying he shouldn't have touched her and all, even after we explained all he did was shake her a little to try to wake her up."

She got up and went over to the stove, smoothing the wrinkles out of her housedress. Returning with a plate of hot apple strudel, she set it in front of Ellie. "I didn't know her except to say hello to. She kept irregular hours, sometimes didn't leave her apartment until midafternoon, other times was up and out before seven a.m." Seeing that Ellie had cutlery and a napkin, she sat down. "She was either dressed to the nines in furs and jewels, or she had jeans and boots on whenever I saw her. I wondered for a while if perhaps she didn't have a job at a racetrack, was a jockey or something, as tiny as she was. But how could she have when she went out at such odd times? I finally decided she just had horses." Behind the thick lenses her eyes looked enormous, her lashes thick and luxurious. She patted her freshly permed white hair, took a troubled bite of her pastry.

"My daughter's picking me up this afternoon. I've decided to spend the night with her and her family. This is all so unsettling."

Ellie nodded sympathetically. "Did Miss Cavanaugh have many visitors, Mrs. Simpson? Did you see people coming and going a lot over there?"

"No," the elderly woman said without hesitation. "The only person I ever saw over there was a big dark haired man, old enough to be her father."

Howard Margolin? Ellie wondered. "Did you ever speak to him?"

Mrs. Simpson shook her head, nose wrinkled distastefully "0h no. I avoided him. He was loud and I disapproved of him, you see. I can't imagine what a pretty girl like her saw in an older man like him. They used to have loud arguments over there that were terrible. I'm not sure if they realized quite how loud they were. Nonetheless they were dreadful. The worst one of all was night before last. I finally had to turn up my television so I couldn't hear."

Ellie leaned forward expectantly. "What was it about?"

Mrs. Simpson looked uncomfortable. "He was accusing her of seeing another man. In the carnal sense. And she was denying it, telling him he was crazy, she wouldn't do that to him, he was her sweetheart and so on." She colored slightly. "It went on and on until I finally considered telling Mr. Holling. But in the end I didn't have to. Sometime during the feature they got quiet. Jimmy Stewart and Doris Day in a spy thriller. I was on the edge of my seat." She forked another bite of strudel into her mouth, followed that with a small sip of tea, then wiped her lips carefully with her paper napkin.

"Did they mention any names? Who he was accusing her of having an affair with?"

Not that she'd heard.

"What about last night?" Ellie persisted. "Did you hear anything last night?"

Margaret shook her head. "To my knowledge he wasn't there. I saw Sue Anne though, twice. First at seven, leaving as I picked up my newspaper in the hall and then coming back about eight. I peeked out just to be sure it was her because I thought I'd heard her a little earlier and was confused."

"And you didn't hear anything again until the music woke you up? No knocking, no doorbell, no talking in the hall?"

Margaret shook her head. "I got plenty of exercise yesterday. Up and down twelve flights of stairs on foot. Good for the heart you know. I'm seventy-eight, though I bet you thought I was a lot younger. Mr. Olson, downstairs, the man I told you about, he guessed I was seventy if I was a day. Though of course he might have been pulling my leg. You never know with men like that."

"Do you know if he's home today?"

"Well, I imagine so," she said. "He's usually there when I knock. Though once or twice when he didn't answer the door, I swear he was in there. Just didn't want to be bothered. You know how men can be . . . "

She winked. "Would you like me to call down and see?"

"No. No thanks," Ellie said. "I'll just check on my way out." She finished her portion of strudel while Mrs. Simpson described how lonely life could be without a man and promised to call again the next time she was in the area before Mrs. Simpson showed her out.

Mr. Olson in 908 took a long time getting to the door. He was a timid-looking little man with a bald head and big mournful eyes whose apartment, when he reluctantly let her in, still contained the touches of a woman—pastel throw pillows on a white couch, a light pink carpet on the floor. Ellie wondered how long the late Mrs. Olson had been gone.

"Three years since Mabel passed," he told her. "And it's a good thing. She'd 'a been scandalized." He shuffled over to a chair, his bedroom slippers looking as dispirited as he did. He, of course, was the man Ellie'd seen in the hallway the night before. Up too late, she decided. He didn't seem to

32

know much about Sue Anne Cavanaugh or Howard Margolin, wasn't positive what either of them looked like, knew them only by the occasional noise they made overhead. "I go to bed early, I get up early," he explained. "Mabel and I, God rest her soul, went to bed every night at ten o'clock and got up at six. For sixty years we followed this schedule." He shook his head sadly. "You see that bird over there?" He pointed with a gnarled finger at a pink ceramic figurine of some species of bird—a robin?— and at Ellie's nod, "That was Mabel's passion."

Ellie smiled. Passion for what? Bird watching? The color pink?

"I broke my routine, stayed up late last night," he said, "dusting all them things of Mabel's. That's why I heard the music, I guess."

Ellie understood what he was talking about after he led her to a back bedroom for a viewing of the collection—at least one hundred figurines of animals, children, plants, landscapes, anything a potter had taken it into his head to create, displayed on dresser tops, in glass cabinets and on shelves, the only common denominator as far as she could determine, the color. Everything was pink, from a shade almost white—a purist would have said it was white—to a dark rose, almost a burgundy.

"This would have taken some time to dust properly," Ellie said, and Mr. Olson nodded wearily.

"That's right. You got it. That's why I didn't go upstairs to see about the music right away." The bed was neatly made, the drapes tightly pulled, and he turned off the bedroom light, carefully closed the door.

"Why do you suppose only you and Mrs. Simpson were bothered by the noise?" Ellie asked.

He cocked his little head. "Place is well built. Noise doesn't carry too far. And half the people who live here don't hear well enough to jump if a bomb went off in the next room." He smiled a little. "I, myself, might not have been bothered, but it boomed so, you know what I mean?" He demonstrated, putting one slippered foot after another down on the pink carpet with an exaggerated step.

"You mean you heard footsteps?"

"No, no. I mean the beat, the rhythm. It boomed. The doorbell rang. Then I heard knocking."

"Knocking? A doorbell? What time was this?"

"I don't know. Twelve maybe. Just as I started dusting." Mr. Olson picked a piece of fluff off his chair and studied it nonchalantly.

"Let me get this straight," Ellie said. "First you thought you heard the doorbell. Did she answer it?"

He shook his head.

"And then you heard knocking?"

He nodded again.

"Did you hear anything else? Make out any conversation?"

He shook his head. "Music was pretty loud."

"So you don't know whether she let whoever it was in or not."

"Nope."

"What about the night before? Did you hear anything out of the ordinary that night?"

A shy smile flitted across the wizened face. "I couldn't make out much of what was said, but there was a beef. A good one. Better than the fights they used to show on television." He rubbed his hands together, made jabbing motions in the air. "Like I said before, it's a good thing Mabel wasn't here. She'd have been scandalized."

That was the sum of what Mr. Olson knew. After the door clicked behind her, Ellie flipped open her notebook. From the sounds of things, whoever had rung the doorbell and then knocked had probably been the murderer. Of course, it was possible someone else had come by after that; but the time was pretty tight, and Mr. Olson hadn't heard anything else.

If, as she suspected, it had been the murderer who knocked, he or she didn't have a key, Ellie suddenly realized.

Elm Hollow was an old neighborhood, midtown, not too far distant from the station. Named for the elm trees that lined the parkways in the area, it had once been one of the most exclusive areas of the city but had been eclipsed by newer developments west of it and was now inhabited primarily by college professors, students, and middle class families who liked the ambience of older homes and were willing to put up with steam heat and window air units, detached garages and tiny yards.

Ellie pulled into the driveway of a smaller brick home on a corner lot, noticing absently that the geraniums in the window boxes needed water. She scooped up the previous evening's *Sentinel* as she crossed the porch and let herself into the one-story rented home. Sparky, her black and white border collie, wagged his tail in greeting. "You need to go outside, don't you boy," she said affectionately and let him out the back door to the fenced in backyard.

The light was flashing on her recorder in the living room, and she listened to her sister Phoebe's slightly nasal twang while she pulled off her jeans. Phoebe sounded excited; Ellie was to call her, immediately.

Ellie washed her face and knotted her long curly hair on top of her head, rifled through her mail, ate a quick piece of toast. Phoebe answered on the first ring.

"I can't believe it," she said breathlessly. "I absolutely cannot believe it. Sue Anne Cavanaugh gets murdered and you cover it."

35

"You talk like you knew her."

"I did. She went to Central. She was in my class. Don't you remember her? Dated Xavier guys from that Catholic boys school. Was real wild?"

Ellie didn't. Two years younger than her sister, she had been in another class in an enormous school. "You're kidding."

"Go get your yearbook," Phoebe commanded. Ellie could hear pages rustling. "Look on page 27."

The book was on the top row of her bookshelf, and she pulled it out, flipping rapidly to the page. Sue Anne Cavanaugh stared back at her, her hair longer, her expression carefree, perhaps a bit coy. Her eyes open instead of closed. Ellie couldn't remember ever seeing her. She read the short paragraph about the girl's school activities. Pep Club sophomore year, a secretarial club her junior year. She picked up the receiver. "Do you remember any friends she had?"

Phoebe thought there'd been a Shirley somebody or other, told her to hold on a minute. Ellie waited, no longer tired. This would be a lead Mitch, even the police, wouldn't get right away.

"Nardo, Shirley Nardo. Page 38."

Ellie turned to page 38 and stared. Dark where Sue Anne was blond, this girl was pretty unremarkable, her hair short and slicked back, her face devoid of expression. The kind of person one passed on the street all the time and never noticed.

"Google her. See if she's still in town."

Ellie grabbed her tablet. There was a Theodore Nardo and a William, but no Shirley.

"One of them could be her father. Try them both. And call me back."

Ellie disconnected her sister and dialed. There was no answer at the Theodore number, and she was telling herself finding Shirley couldn't be so easy when a woman, her voice sounding tired and indifferent, picked up the phone at the William number. "What's that? You're looking for Shirley? Hold on a minute." A few seconds later she was back. "Shirley just moved again," she said in her tired voice. "I was looking for her number." She read it off slowly, a local number that, by the prefix, might be downtown. She didn't ask Ellie who she was or why she wanted her daughter's phone number.

Her own mother wouldn't have dreamt of supplying her number to a disembodied voice on the telephone, Ellie thought as she punched in the numbers the woman had given her. It would be courting disaster.

There was no answer.

At least she still lived in town, Ellie thought, hanging up. At least she hadn't joined the mecca of high school graduates who had hot-footed it out the minute they had diploma in hand. She let Sparky in, fed him, and put fresh water in his bowl. After that she filled the bathtub for a much needed soak. She could feel the tension and fatigue of the last fourteen hours dissipate in the steam as she lay back, eyes closed. Central. The murdered girl had gone to Central, had attended classes with the same teachers she had, had known some of the same people. Ellie wished she could remember her or her friend, get some picture of what they'd been like. But she'd been too busy back then with school work and soccer, journalism and debate, to notice girls in Phoebe's class, especially the kind who dated parochial school boys. They had a tendency never to participate in Central activities, to prefer their boyfriends' sporting events over those of their home school.

Maybe the murderer would turn out to be one of them, a Catholic boy from Xavier. Some guy who'd dated her and been dumped for this older man, what was his name, Margolin, she'd been hearing about. It was possible. An Army recruit, maybe, who'd gone on a three year rotation only to come back and find his position supplanted by a man old enough to be his father. Or maybe Sue Anne had gotten involved in some drug scam, was dealing out of her apartment. Sgt. McDaniel's reaction to her question about that came to mind. Just what had he seen in the bedroom? Perhaps the girl had owed big money to someone and been unable to come up with it when it came due.

Ten to one it was Margolin, common sense told her as she lifted the drain with her big toe. Why get dramatic about the whole thing? Most victims in situations like this were killed by a spouse or boyfriend. Everybody knew that. Whatever the case, idle conjecture would get her nowhere. She drew on a clean pair of jeans and searched through her closet for a favorite shirt. She would have to piece the thing out, bit by bit, as she uncovered facts. And she could only do that by getting out there and talking to people. Fred Burrow's question about when she'd sleep had been a good one, she realized now, trying to stifle a yawn. Just when was she going to get to close her eyes? She had twenty minutes to get back to work.

"Guard the place," she told Sparky and headed out the door . . .

Mitch, she saw, had gone home. A note on her desk in his careful script told her to meet him in the morning for a nine o'clock press briefing at police headquarters. He had underlined 'don't be late.' Ellie crumbled up the note, then caught Fred Burrows eyeing her through the glass walls of his office. She smiled.

After straightening up her desk, she checked the assignment sheet. There, sandwiched between city council debate and big name rock concert assignments was her name by

"Safety Expert Demonstration on Fireworks Disposal," 7:00 p.m., Benson Hall parking lot.

"Somebody's got to do it," Barkley Houston said smoothly, studying the sheet over her shoulder. "The Fourth of July will be here before you know it."

And assignment in hell will be here before you know it, Ellie thought, with your name by it. She covered the fireworks safety demonstration, turned in her tape and was sent out to cover a personal injury accident or P.I. as they referred to it in the news room at 90th and Southern. This is getting ridiculous, she thought. Why me? Why tonight? The light changed on Wilmette, and she followed the cars in front of hers, wishing the Volkswagen had air conditioning. P.I.'s were even worse than domestics. What was newsworthy about them? Who cared to gape at such tragedy before going to bed at night? The public, she'd been assured by several reporters. They'd been fed a steady diet of it and grown accustomed.

The accident scene, when she arrived, was quiet, orderly. A seventy-year-old man had driven his Ford over the curb, across the lawn and into a tree at 9020 Southern; police suspected the man had suffered a coronary and paramedics were working on his inert form in the grass, trying to stabilize him before transporting him to St. Alberts.

Ellie got the requisite video: the paramedics with the victim, the mangled Ford wrapped around the tree, patrolmen directing slow-moving cars past the rescue squad, then headed back to the station. She'd call St. Alberts for an update on the man's condition prior to recording.

When 11:00 came and went and her cohorts had streamed out, leaving her to her own devices in the newsroom, she pulled out the scrap of paper with the phone number on it, grabbed a telephone near the police radio and sat down.

Shirley Nardo answered on the second ring, sounding high on something, or drunk.

"I told Sue Anne not to have anything to do with Howard Margolin," the murdered girl's friend said. "He was too old for her, he had kids her age for crissakes. But would Sue Anne listen? Hell no. She saw the money and ran. Now look what it's got her. The bastard killed her. Why haven't they arrested him yet? That's what I want to know."

Ellie heard ice cubes clinking in a glass, tried to picture the girl in her yearbook photo as she would look now, eight years later.

"What do you know about him? Have you met him?"

Shirley sighed. "I've seen him a couple of times. Looks like a gorilla in a suit, know what I mean? But I haven't talked to him."

"Why's that?"

"Because he didn't approve of me. He didn't think I was a good influence on Sue Anne. Doesn't that beat all?" There was a dark silence. Then, sounding a little less tough: "Sue Anne and I were like sisters, close, you know? We depended on each other. Lived over on Decker in an apartment we fixed up, worked, partied a lot. Then she met Margolin, let him set her up in that fancy place. If she hadn't met him, she'd still be alive, we'd probably still live there." Her voice trailed off.

"When did you last see her or talk to her?"

"She called me one night, late, a couple of weeks ago, high as a kite. Went on and on about some damn horse show she was going to, or she'd just been to. I don't remember. She was into horses, you know, after the creep bought her a couple. Practically lived out at some stable somewhere." She didn't have any idea where the stable was located or who owned it. "Sue Anne changed after she was around Margolin a while," she explained. "Bragged about her trips and her jewels and her horses and all until I just tuned her out, quit paying attention. She didn't love him, you understand. I don't think she even liked him. But she was in hog heaven living in that apartment, buying all the clothes she wanted, going to Bermuda and god-knows where all. Who wouldn't have been?"

Ellie cleared her throat. "Do you know anything about his family? You mentioned he'd been married."

"He has a wife somewhere. An ex-wife I should say, and a couple of kids, grown-up, married. I don't know where any of 'em are. Sue Anne just mentioned them once. I think they live somewhere else."

"What about her family? Are they around?"

"Yeah, they're in town. But if you're wondering what they thought of Margolin, I don't know. Sue Anne got to where she lied a lot the last couple of years. Howie's influence, I suppose. She told me they thought he was great, but I didn't believe it." She sighed loudly, and Ellie heard the ice cubes clinking again.

"Would Sue Anne have told you about it, if say, she and Mr. Margolin had a fight, or she was having second thoughts about him, thinking of leaving him, that sort of thing?"

"No way." Shirley was emphatic though she was beginning to slur her words. "Things haven't been the same with us the last couple of years. She didn't talk to me about stuff like that. She'd call me every once in a while with a 'hi, how are ya, whatchadoing,' and then she'd have to go, Howie was coming over. I was just somebody to call when she was bored or really stoned."

Ellie was about to follow up on that when a doorbell buzzed in the background.

"Hey, hold on a sec, somebody's here," Shirley said. There were the faint sounds of people talking, and then Shirley was back. "It's Bobby, my friend, here to cheer me up. Isn't that nice?" She whispered something to him, then laughed mirthlessly. "I'm talking to a rePORter," she said. "Really. From a television station. You don't believe me, talk to her yourself." They argued. Ellie got the impression the phone was passed back and forth three or four times while Shirley laughed and Bobby swore. Then Shirley came back on again. "Whaddya say your name was?"

She repeated her name, and Shirley relayed it to Bobby.

"Ain't never heard of her," Ellie thought he replied.

"Listen, Shirley," Ellie said loudly. "Let me ask you one more question, and I'll let you go."

"What's that?"

"Did Sue Anne date anybody in the past who might have done this? I'm wondering about former boyfriends. Say an old boyfriend she dumped, or somebody she wouldn't go out with, someone like that."

She should have known the answer without asking, she thought cynically as the police radio came alive with a crackle and the dispatcher, in surprisingly clear tones, announced a personal injury accident in the westernmost suburb of Maplewood.

"Sue Anne had plenty of boyfriends," Shirley replied flatly. "And half of 'em would just a soon have killed her as looked at her. She got tired of 'em fast, you know what I mean? Especially when they didn't spend enough money on her. But Margolin did it. I'd bet my life on it. Besides, he was the only man she saw the last couple of years, far as I know. Anybody else so much as looked at her, he'd have killed 'em."

As if covering that car accident hadn't been enough, Ellie, finally at home with Sparky, had a message on her answering machine. This one was from Janice, her contact at the dog rescue organization she helped out when she could. Janice needed her services for a German shepherd. Ellie punched in the address on her computer and saw that it was about five miles south and east of her. Hmmm. Now she was wide awake again. She went into the bedroom, pulled out some black jeans and a black t-shirt, and donned them quickly. Then she headed down to the basement, Sparky in tow, and selected a couple of tools she put in a dark canvas bag.

"Sorry I have to leave again, boy," she said to the black and white dog as she let herself out of the house. She liked to think Sparky understood.

She drove the quiet streets quickly and found the address with no trouble: a wood-frame single story house with a screened in, well-lit front porch, but no lights in the back. She circled the block, found the alley behind the row of houses, and pulled in. Three garages from the house she parked her car.

Gravel crunched under her feet as she made her way toward the backyard. A cat screeched somewhere in the darkness, and she heard some loud voices arguing from an upstairs window in the second house she passed before she got to the backyard she sought. She paused, gazed at the house, then quietly opened a gate in the page fence and let herself into the yard. She could see an old dog house to her right, flanking the fence, and she tiptoed toward it, praying the dog wouldn't bark.

The poor thing didn't make a sound. It lay on the ground and barely managed to lift its head in greeting. Ellie dropped down on her knees, gave the animal a reassuring pat on the head. Dog feces lay everywhere and she breathed through her mouth. She could faintly see that the dog was collared and chained to a stake in the ground, and, after she pulled out a collar and leash of her own and looped it around the creature's thin neck, she unbuckled the original collar and dropped it on the ground. She wasn't sure if the dog could stand, but it got shakily to its feet and she coaxed it to follow.

Dog and woman made their way painstakingly to the open gate and out of the yard, Ellie holding her breath and the dog breathing hard. No lights came on in the house, and they continued down the alley slowly and quietly. She would have liked to pick the poor creature up—he was skin and bones—but he was a large dog so she didn't. When they finally reached the car, she opened the passenger door and helped the dog in, closed the door softly, hurried around to the driver's door, got in, and drove away. It wasn't until she'd driven out of the immediate neighborhood that she pulled over and offered the dog some water. The dog cast what she thought were grateful eyes on her, lapped dispiritedly, and put its head back down on the seat.

She couldn't take the dog to her house, she decided. This poor thing needed more care than she knew how to give. She flipped out her phone and called Janice. Janice was a nurse and could monitor the dog, get him to a vet if necessary.

A short time later she and the woman were helping the dog out of the car and into Janice's house. Neither of them said much. "Cruel bastards," Janice muttered, referring to the owners, and Ellie nodded. She headed home, and when Sparky greeted her at the door, she gave him a big hug.

# CHAPTER FIVE

The voice was businesslike, monotonous, the words jargon from another world. "Hyoid bone crushed, windpipe collapsed . . . no air to the lungs . . . contusions to the cervical area consistent with steady, crushing force . . ."

Detective Bieterman, reading from the autopsy report, didn't look bored exactly, just tired.

"They like to read the reports to cover their asses," Mitch had explained earlier. "That way if we screw it up it isn't their fault."

"Blood tests indicate high levels of alcohol and the opioid hydrocodone, more commonly referred to as Vicodin" —he quoted percentages— "contents of the stomach were minimal . . ."

Standing behind the front desk of the police press room, papers arranged neatly in front of him, he could have passed as a college professor delivering a lecture if it hadn't been for the content of his speech and the audience sitting at the old metal desks taking notes. In addition to Ellie and Mitch, two television reporters, three radio newsmen, and two newspaper reporters had straggled in exchanging quips about the rotten hot weather and nodding grudgingly at Ellie when Mitch introduced her around. One of them was the guy from the *Sentinel* she'd talked to the night of the murder. Hancock. She caught his eye and nodded.

"The Medical Examiner puts the time of death between eleven-thirty and one a.m. There were no signs of a struggle, no signs of a forced entry, nothing to indicate any violence prior to the actual murder . . ."

Mitch was taking notes on her left and for a fleeting moment she was glad they were working as a team; this left her the opportunity to soak it all in, develop impressions, listen for nuances in the detective's delivery. Unfortunately, Det. Bieterman seemed to be a pro at the noncommittal, abridged press release; there weren't even body motions to judge, his arms slack at his sides except when he flipped to a new page, his eyebrows, the creases around his mouth hardly moving.

"We appreciate your interest in keeping the public informed, and we'll let you know of any pertinent developments as they arise," he said in summation. His eyes swept the room impatiently, paused a millisecond when he saw Ellie.

There was a slight flurry of activity from the audience.

"Any promising leads detective?" This from one of the radio guys in the back.

"I won't comment on that."

Mitch shook his head knowingly at Ellie as if to say that meant no. He spoke up. "What about the murder weapon? Was there a garrote, or did the murderer use his hands?"

"No comment, Mr. Bassman."

"What about physical evidence? A champagne glass with fingerprints all over it? Some telltale keys? A note in a foreign hand?" Appreciative laughter erupted in the room as the detective stuffed his paperwork into a manila folder and hiked his suit coat off the back of his chair.

"Sounds like you're a mystery novel fan," he said with a slight grin. Then he left.

Mitch looked at Ellie. During the drive over he'd warned her about Det. Bieterman. The guy was difficult to work with, he said, avoided the press, gave only the barest of details during press releases. "Why the hell couldn't Parson have been given this case," Mitch said now as he and Ellie joined the mass exodus out the door. "He'd help us out."

"Why don't you go talk to Parson," Ellie said. "Maybe he heard something." Parson, she knew, was another homicide detective, and Mitch's main contact.

Mitch looked skeptical but tossed her his car keys. At least they could have some coffee, bitch about the weather. "I'll be back in fifteen minutes," he said. "Don't disappear."

Ellie couldn't believe she'd gotten rid of him so easily. The elevators to the second floor and the homicide department proved easy enough to find. But the rotund and officious-looking sergeant parked by them was a barrier she hadn't counted on.

"I'd like to speak to Det. Bieterman," she said firmly. "About the Cavanaugh case."

He picked up his phone, talked briefly to someone, replaced it. He looked surprised. "Take the elevator to the second floor. Detective's office is at the end on your right."

Bieterman was on the phone when she looked in the open door; he motioned her to a seat facing him, rummaged among the papers on his desk for one, found it, read it off. It sounded like something about overtime hours.

The office was small and cluttered. In addition to the disarray on his desk, several metal cabinet drawers behind him stood open, each bulging with its own odd assortment of manila folders and scraps of paper; the cabinet tops housed foot tall stacks; and the whole mess looked like it could come down if someone slammed the door hard. There was nothing of a personal nature. Take out the office clutter, wipe off his fingerprints, and all traces of his presence would be gone in a matter of minutes. He was around forty, she decided; there was a faint blue shadow on his face, his eyes were

47

slightly bloodshot, and he had a small scar under his left eye she hadn't noticed. He looked capable, the no-nonsense type who cut people off if they got long-winded, and she remembered that when he got off the phone, turning his inscrutable stare on her.

"I have some information about the Cavanaugh murder you might be able to use," she said. Quickly, she recounted her conversations with the dead girl's neighbors, and how she had located the ex-roommate, Shirley Nardo. "The fight the neighbors overheard between Miss Cavanaugh and Howard Margolin the night before she was murdered could prove significant," she pointed out, "and it may be that Shirley Nardo knows more than she's admitting to me. It's worth checking out at any rate."

He nodded. She thought she saw the hint of a smile behind the tired eyes.

"What I'd like to work out," she said when he remained silent, "is a deal with you. What say you keep me informed about things if I do the same for you?" She was afraid he'd simply say no or want to get into why she was so interested in the case, what she possibly hoped to gain by taking such an active role in the investigation, but he didn't.

"I figured that was why you were here," he merely said. "I'll think about it. But I'll warn you upfront, I've had some rotten experiences with journalists before and I'm wary. You know the guy you were sitting with in the briefing . . . Bassman?"

Ellie nodded.

"He's not one of my favorite reporters."

Ellie didn't get a chance to ask him why not. "You're new, aren't you?" he asked.

Ellie explained she'd been covering the graveyard shift the last six months, and he hadn't seen her before because of that.

**48**

"You experienced enough to know when I'm telling you something off the record, or something I don't want anybody to hear?"

She nodded, trying not to look exasperated.

"When I say nobody, you realize I mean nobody . . . not your news director, not Bassman, not even your mother?" he persisted.

Ellie assured him she understood, feeling like a school girl called on the carpet.

He loosened his tie and fixed her with a serious look. He yanked a file out of one of the cabinets and dumped it on his desk. It was bulging. "Let's see here. Where do we stand at this point?" In a sort of verbal shorthand, he abridged what he read. The Cavanaugh family was straight, pretty broken up about the whole thing, but cooperative. It was a large Catholic family, eight kids, St. Francis Parish, and from the way the father talked, the youngest daughter had been an embarrassment, not married, without employment, living off an older man. They'd never actually met Howard Margolin, but they continued to see the daughter, albeit infrequently.

Margolin, the boyfriend, he continued, was clean, had no priors, and owned a well-known restaurant and lounge on Belvedere called the Catamaran. According to some sources he cheated big on his income taxes, ran with some sleazy people, but even if it was true, that didn't mean he was the one. Several of his employees verified that on the night of the murder he'd stayed at the lounge until after 2:00 a.m., giving him a pretty good alibi.

The crime scene hadn't yielded much. No fingerprints, just a few fibers they'd sent to the lab. Through the manager, Mr. Holling, they'd learned that the apartment was rented to Margolin, who had never lived there but had made frequent visits over the last two years. The Cavanaugh woman's movements the last day of her life were still sketchy. Other than a call from a kid at a pharmacy on Wiltshire and 96th who'd recognized her picture in the paper and said he was sure she was the one he'd sold cigarettes to around seven-thirty or eight that evening, and the elderly neighbor, Margaret Simpson's sightings, they had nothing. Bieterman's partner, Det. Morrison, had looked into her daily activities and learned that she spent a considerable amount of time at a stable just past Milvern near the river. They'd interviewed a Jerry Norgaard, the owner, but he claimed not to have seen her the last day of her life. "Unless someone comes forward, we'll have to conclude she stayed in, didn't go anywhere else," Bieterman said.

The phone rang and he picked it up. Ellie thought of the Cavanaugh household while she waited. With only one older sister herself, it was hard to imagine what it must have been like growing up in a family that big, sharing clothes, rooms, the whole thing. Had Sue Anne become claustrophobic as she suspected she would have, anxious to get away from so many people? Or had she received no attention from parents worn out by so many children? Maybe it was just the opposite—maybe she'd been spoiled, doted on by all of them and as a consequence felt she was owed a living. What was even harder to imagine was how anyone could be satisfied spending her days working on a tan, riding her horse, having her fingernails done. It would fry the brain. Speaking of which . . .

"What about the drug angle?" she asked when the detective concluded his call. "Have you made any headway in that area?"

"Not yet," he said. "But we're looking into it. Somebody was supplying her." With what he wouldn't say, though it wasn't hard to figure out. From the evidence she'd just heard about via the autopsy, Sue Anne had had plenty of everything.

"Shirley Nardo told me Howard Margolin had been married before and there were children. Do you have any idea where they might be?"

"In Arizona," he replied. "According to Margolin, the divorce was amicable, happened long before he met the Cavanaugh woman, and he still sends money to his ex-wife each month even though the children are grown and married. In fact, he's a grandfather. We'll check it all out of course."

"It doesn't look like there'd be any motive for the ex-wife to kill her then?"

"Doesn't seem to be."

Margolin was the prime suspect, Ellie concluded, watching him close the file and lean back in his chair. The only suspect from what she could tell. Talk had centered almost exclusively on him, from the sounds of it much investigative work had already been conducted into his professional and private life, and there was the evidence of that fight between the couple the night before Sue Anne was murdered. What had that been about again? Oh yes, Sue Anne's alleged affair with someone else. What about that, she asked. Had they turned up anything that suggested there was truth to those allegations?

He shook his head and smiled. Why was it she got the impression all of a sudden that he wasn't leveling with her? He had read through the notes in his folder quickly, assuredly, hadn't seemed to be leaving anything out. He had looked surprised, sort of, when she'd told him about the fight. Had he known all along? Were they already, he and Morrison, making lists of who could have been having a secret affair with Sue Anne under Margolin's nose? Suddenly she wasn't so sure Margolin was the prime suspect.

"He is," Mitch said huffily after five minutes of uncomfortable silence while the air conditioner in his car blew loudly. Fuming by his locked Chrysler where she'd found him when she'd suddenly recalled he was waiting for her, he was only now beginning to talk. "It looks to me like Margolin murdered her, then copped the pearls to scam the insurance people and throw the cops off the scent."

"Pearls? What pearls?"

"Oh, didn't I tell you? A ten thousand dollar pearl necklace was ripped off at the murder scene." He adjusted his rearview mirror and gave her a superior look.

"Where'd you hear this? Parson?"

He nodded. "Off the record you understand. We can't put it in a story yet. Cops always try to withhold stuff only the murderer would know so when he mentions it in his confession they know they got the right man. Oh, and the creep used his hands, wore gloves. No garrote, no fingerprints." He maneuvered around a stalled truck and blasted his horn at a skinny puppy about to put a tiny paw into the street. "Where were you by the way?"

Withholding evidence from her wasn't the same as lying, Ellie reasoned uncertainly, but she didn't like learning about the missing necklace or the gloves from Mitch instead of Bieterman. They were supposed to come clean with one another, not omit important details.

"In Bieterman's office," she said absently. "I thought it would be a good idea to touch base with him." Ellie missed the stunned look he gave her, lost in thought.

"Male chauvinist's my guess," he muttered after a while. "Hitting on you . . . only reason I can think of why he let you in. I'm sure he didn't tell you anything we can use."

It took a while for it to sink in he was talking about Bieterman. Ellie decided to ignore him. But it left her wondering exactly why Bieterman had agreed to talk to her. And it occurred to her that if he was withholding details from her, she would be smart to withhold a few details from him in the future.

"What's the problem between Mitch and that homicide detective?" she asked Barkley Houston later when Mitch wasn't around.

Barkley grinned. "Mitch made the mistake of doing a piece on the homicide department a few years ago where he quoted Bieterman criticizing his boss about something. Took a while for Mitch to get anybody in the cop shop to talk to him after that. Burrows almost had to reassign him."

Well, she had something working in her favor, she thought, suppressing a grin. No wonder Mitch had been so unhappy. She now had a direct line to the primary investigator, an advantage he'd never hope to have. Not that Bieterman was telling her everything, she thought, sobering.

# CHAPTER SIX

Ellie almost overshot the turn, hidden in dense foliage. The farmhouse, set back in the trees, had a big screen porch and a privacy fence on the north side she suspected hid a swimming pool. The yard was well-tended, and flowers bloomed in carefully laid out beds. Someone had turned on a sprinkler, and it undulated slowly while birds tittered in the glistening grass.

Owning a stable must be profitable, she thought as she coasted around the back. A woman weeding in a garden looked up casually, then went back to work.

Fifty yards down the drive was the barn. Norgaard Stables a sign in large black letters announced. Ringed by half a dozen metal pens and an arena, the white structure had a steeply-pitched roof, and was connected by an open-air breezeway to a smaller metal shed of some sort that looked as though it had been tacked on as an afterthought.

Two chocolate labradors by now lapped her car barking loudly, and Ellie paused in the act of getting out, not sure she wanted to find out whether they meant business. Fortunately, the owner, Jerry Norgaard, appeared at the barn entrance and called to them. Both dogs trotted obediently toward him, pink tongues lolling, while Ellie got out of her car.

"Here about that mare?" he called.

"Not exactly . . ."

They could talk in his office, he decided, acquiescing reluctantly to an interview after she introduced herself. He led her through the deep shavings in the aisle under ten pairs of watchful eyes while Ellie tried not to wrinkle her nose at the unaccustomed smell.

"Who was that?" she asked Norgaard when they were seated in his office, referring to a scruffy-looking man she'd passed in the aisle. He'd come out of a tack room, several Navaho blankets under his arm and a saddle slung over one shoulder; he'd leered faintly at her when she'd looked back.

"Bart Vogel, friend of mine," Norgaard offered. He took off his hat. His face was tanned and weathered except for a pale horizontal stripe extending across his forehead, and Ellie suspected the tan on his neck and hands ended at the collar and cuffs of his long-sleeved cotton shirt. If there was a pool behind the privacy fence, he didn't use it. Except perhaps by moonlight.

"He work for you?"

"No. Only Rich L'Heureux does," the man said promptly. "He's out in the arena right now working a horse for me. But he's more family than anything else." He leaned back in his chair, looking as if even that much conversation pained him. "So, what do you want to know? I've already told the police everything they asked."

Ellie gave him her friendliest grin. "I'm aware of that. And I promise not to waste your time. I'm just doing a little nosing around on my own, and when I heard Miss Cavanaugh rode horses, I had to come out and look around for myself, you understand."

He didn't look as if he did understand, but he didn't say anything.

"I was wondering if you'd mind telling me how Miss Cavanaugh happened to keep her horse here . . . "

"Howard Margolin," he said shortly. "The woman's boyfriend. Came out a few years back, bought a gray mare and a yellow gelding and hired me to teach her to ride. Adults usually have a hell of a time learning that late, but she was determined, and she did pretty well."

"I take it Mr. Margolin didn't share her interest?"

Norgaard smiled at this and shook his head. "He wasn't hardly the type. I gathered he was only keeping her happy by buying the horses. He's a busy man."

"Did you get the impression they were happy together?"

"I'm busy myself," he said shortly. "Five colts in training, eight students, forty head boarded here. Doesn't leave me much time to know how my clients get along in their personal lives." He stared at her cooly. "About all I can tell you is that she took to riding pretty quick, and she went to the shows with the bunch of us last year and this spring. She seemed like a nice-enough young woman. We didn't know her real well, but we were shocked to hear what happened to her. We're just hoping now to hear the police have made an arrest, picked up whoever did it, gets him off the street."

"If it's a him."

"What's that?

"If it's a him."

"Oh, well. Right." He stared at her.

"When was the last time you saw her?"

"Friday morning. About eight. Worked her mare and the yellow horse, left about eleven."

"Did you talk to her?"

He sat for a moment as if trying to recall. "No. I'm starting a little filly, and I've had my hands full the last couple of days. We just waved. No conversation."

"What about Saturday night? The police don't seem to

be very sure of her whereabouts . . . Could she have been out here, even briefly?"

Norgaard shook his head. "I hear every car that passes the house, and my wife and I were here all night. Watered about eleven and went to bed. There wasn't anybody out." He gave her an impatient look as if to say she'd promised she wouldn't take much of his time.

"Would you mind if I walked around, talked to some of your clients?" she asked.

There was a flicker of something—doubt?—annoyance? but he shrugged, said he supposed it would be okay if she thought it might help. "But I do have a lot of work to do," he said.

She followed him back through the thick piles of shaving, nodding appreciatively as he pointed out the tack rooms, the feed bins, the lounge. He wasn't going to let her just wander, it appeared: they were embarking on a guided tour.

A young girl hosing down her horse in the shower room smiled, then turned back as the animal spun skittishly, its hooves reverberating loudly on the wet cement. That was Quinn Farrell, Norgaard said, one of his students.

The metal building she'd taken for a large shed turned out to be an indoor arena. Standing by the trainer in the sandy-bottomed structure, she breathed in large whiffs of the fresh air blowing through the breezeway door while a young man in the center of the arena walked in circles with a horse trotting around him, attached to him by a long line of rope snapped to the horse's halter.

"He's longeing him," Norgaard explained. "Wearing him down a little before I ride him." The horse was jet-black, flecked with white lather from a hard workout, but even to Ellie's inexperienced eye, it was plain the animal had plenty of spirit left. It trotted briskly, its gleaming neck arched, its tail extended slightly. When L'Heureux led the horse toward them, its sides heaving in and out like a bellows, its nostrils flared, Ellie reached out a tentative hand to stroke it.

"He's full of it today," L'Heureux said admiringly. "I'd get on the son-of-a-buck before he gets his second wind if I were you."

"Miss Schimmel is a television reporter," Norgaard said to the younger man. "She's here about Sue Anne."

They exchanged looks and Rich stopped smiling.

"It's hard to believe she's been murdered," he said soberly to Ellie. "I hope the police have some idea who did it." Youthful looking, with myriad freckles on his face and arms, he was a little older than she, Ellie judged.

"No doubt they do," she said cheerfully.

Norgaard cleared his throat a little, and the three of them stood judging one another silently; Norgaard and L'Heureux against Ellie. The horse soon tired of this; not wanting to remain still, he swung around, almost clipping Ellie as he went by.

"There, what'd I say," Rich said after he had the beast under control again. "He's already got his second wind back."

Norgaard, with obvious reluctance, took the length of rope. "Better see to that yellow horse on the walker," he said pointedly to Rich as he led the horse back through the breezeway. "He's cooled out by now."

"Norgaard's riled," Rich explained when he'd disappeared. "He's not much of a talker on a good day, and the police have been out a couple of times asking questions. I suspect, too, he's afraid it'll hurt business."

The two of them set off across the arena, emerging on the far side into the brilliant sun.

"Sue Anne was a wild one, liked to flirt a bit, but I didn't ever think it would come to this," he said when Ellie asked him to characterize the dead girl. "She'd never pick up strangers, that kind of stuff. Fact, she was pretty cautious. One of

**58**

the things she liked best about her apartment, she told me, was the security guard."

They'd come to the walker, and he switched off the metal contraption, untied the horse that had been patiently circling around it. "Made her feel safe, the security guard," he said as they headed back into the barn, the horse between them. "Course that could have been Sue Anne bragging, wanting us to know she lived in such a ritzy place. For all I know there wasn't any security guard but . . ."

"You're saying then, the murderer was probably someone she knew. Someone who had access to her apartment?"

"I don't know about that, the access part, but someone she knew, yes. Had to be. Like I said, she flirted a lot, but she was cautious."

"Who'd she flirt with?"

"Everybody," he said, rolling his eyes. "Guys at the horse shows, me, why even Bart Vogel. You meet him? It was in her nature I guess. Nobody took it seriously, though. Everybody knew about Margolin. 'Don't mess with Howie,' Sue Anne always said, 'unless you think messing with matches in a hay barn in the middle of July is fun.' She loved to be surrounded by guys, but she was smart. Margolin was where the money was, and she knew that." He stopped in front of an open stall door, tapped the horse on the rump and slid the door shut after the horse went inside. "Here . . . give him this," he said when the horse nosed through the metal bars and nuzzled at Ellie's outstretched hand. He produced a small piece of carrot, showed her how to flatten her palm so the horse wouldn't bite her accidentally. She could barely feel it when the animal took the carrot.

"Somehow I'm reminded of Little Red Riding Hood," Ellie said when the animal, worrying the carrot, drew its lips back, revealing long, stained teeth.

Rich laughed. "That's why you have to be careful, do it

the right way." He shoved away from the wall and at the soda pop machine stopped. "Want something?"

"No thanks."

"Suit yourself." He thumped the machine and pulled out a can of orange soda.

"Tell me about Bart Vogel," Ellie suggested when they'd taken seats on a bench nearby. "Why'd you say 'even with him,' when you were talking about who Sue Anne flirted with?"

"Did I?" L'Heureux grinned. "Force of habit, I guess. Vogel and I don't get along very well."

Ellie had to coax the why out of him.

Vogel had been sponging off Jerry Norgaard, was the way he put it, for close to six months, ever since he'd been caught down in Oklahoma abusing a string of horses he was being paid to train by a wealthy guy there. Tying their heads up before shows and depriving them of water so they'd keep their heads down in the ring, getting a crooked veterinary friend of his to deaden tails so they couldn't swish at flies. "And now he's up here conning a couple of people into giving him their horses," he said, frowning. "Of course he isn't abusing them like he was down there, but he never rides them. Scared to, I think. Just longes them, turns them out in the pens, and sticks his poor, sucker clients up on their backs. It's a wonder somebody hasn't been killed. Doesn't give Jerry a dime either. Always stealing equipment." The frown deepened. "Talk about taking advantage of an old friendship. But for some reason women are attracted to him. Even Sue Anne. Though like I said before, it was all a game to her. Didn't mean anything." He sighed, then grinned. "You know, I'd have to say I liked Sue Anne. In spite of her gold-digging and all, she was a fun person. Never hurt anybody either. It's still hard to believe somebody killed her."

"How'd you find out about it?"

"Jerry. Heard it on the radio."

"What'd you do Saturday night?"

"Partied."

"Who'd you party with?"

"Some friends of mine. Couple who lives next door to me. Went to the Mexican place in Milvern, drank margaritas." He rolled his eyes at the memory. "Woke up feeling like I was dead, then come to find out about Sue Anne. What a day."

Ellie wondered idly if he still got asked to produce identification when he went to the bars.

He told a few anecdotes about Sue Anne, was in the middle of a story about how Sue Anne had convinced Margolin to buy her not one but two silver inlaid saddles when over the music from the radio they heard Norgaard's low voice. "Rich," he called, sounding impatient, "get me a lead rope off Pecos door."

L'Heureux winked at Ellie, looking a little embarrassed. "Sorry. Guess I gotta go. Finish that story some other time, okay?"

He reminded her a little of a grown-up Tom Sawyer, she thought, as he headed in the direction of Norgaard's voice, and she set off in search of Bart Vogel.

He looked like one of Charles Russell's cowboys on the greeting cards her father mailed to his fellow Harvard alumni back east every year. Ellie waited patiently for him to circle the arena. "Chuck the three-piece suits if you're contemplating a visit," her father would write his friends. "We're men in the midwest."

Evidently he knew who she was and what she wanted, she thought as she clambered up on the fence for a better view. The horse swished its tail and took slow steps while Vogel looked off in the other direction, studiously avoiding her.

A mosquito lit on her arm and she smacked it. When she looked up he was staring at her. She waved. Caught, he waved back.

"She was going with that Margolin dude. I don't think we talked to each other more than two or three times," he muttered when finally he reached her and Ellie asked how well he knew Sue Anne. "Besides I'm busy most of every day. I got horses to train." Both of them gazed at the old brown nag he sat on, cropping at the tufts of grass under the fence.

"Is this by any chance one of them?" Ellie asked.

"Nah, this is Babe," he replied affectionately, failing to grasp the intended barb. "She's as old as dirt, been with me forever." He pet her neck, and the old mare closed an eye, continued to chew quietly.

"Let's see, you've been here about six months, but you didn't get to know her all that well. Is that what you're saying?"

He nodded, looking stubborn. "That's about the size of it, Miss."

Ellie felt rivulets of sweat dripping down her back and looked longingly in the direction of the privacy fence barely visible down the lane. What would they all think if she vaulted the fence, plunged into the pool? A colorful movement on the edge of her vision drew her attention. It was the woman she'd seen as she drove in, still out in her garden. Mrs. Norgaard?

"Norgaard told me you were an old friend of his," she said, turning back to Vogel. "What about his wife? Are you an old friend of hers, too?"

He smiled, hugely. "I knew Barbara before I ever laid eyes on Jerry. She was a beauty. Long tail of red hair, temper to match. Rode barrel racers, led the country in points for a while." He sighed. "But then she met Norgaard, got married, settled down. She ain't much fun anymore. Never see her over at the barn. That's what happens when women get hitched. All the play goes out of them." He gazed off in her direction shaking his head wistfully. "Too bad marriage was ever invented, I say."

Ellie asked him his whereabouts the previous Saturday.

"Went to an auction," he replied. "In Sioux Falls."

"Buy anything?"

"Nope." He smiled. "Buddy and me drove up there for the hell of it. Met up with a couple of women, closed the bars. I didn't get back till Sunday morning. Heard about the murder here. Everybody was shocked."

"They were upset, eh? Everyone talking about it."

"You could say that. They all knew her a lot better than me. She'd been around a couple of years, dontcha know." And that was all he would say. Questions about Norgaard were met with one syllable answers; his past escapades were explained away as simple misunderstandings; and a reference to missing equipment brought a blank look.

She was wasting her time, Ellie thought as Vogel, eyes half-closed, slumped back in the saddle. The horse was asleep, she concluded: both eyes were closed, and it was listing, one side cozying up against the fence.

"Hey there, git up," Bart said when the pressure of the wood slat grew uncomfortable against his leg. He kicked at the animal's underbelly with the heel of his boot and an eye opened. "She's some beast, isn't, she?" he said.

Could have said the same about the man, Ellie thought.

"I saw you drive in," Barbara Norgaard said. "I thought you were here to buy a horse . . ." Her hands were caked with drying mud, each fingernail framed in the brown muck; and Ellie watched as she dug a hole in the ground, filled it with water from a garden hose and plopped a plant into it. She worked carefully, shoveling the dirt back into the watery hole with a trowel, pressing it down with her small loafered foot. "If you give them plenty of water they don't go into shock," she explained, standing back to survey her work with one eye closed. "Though it is hot, and late . . ."

The garden was laid out in a haphazard fashion, wild flowers flanking beds of carefully tended annuals and perennials. From a distance it looked like an impressionist painting, and Ellie thought of her drooping geraniums with shame. "Jerry says if the garden grows much more there won't be room for the barn in a few years," the woman said with a smile. "But flowers are my passion."

Ellie let her talk shop for a while and then brought up the purpose for her visit. "I hope the police haven't been trampling through here investigating this murder the last few days."

"Oh no," she said. "They've only been out the one time to talk to Jerry. Or was it two?" She stopped, brushed back an auburn curl tinged with gray and narrowed her eyes. Perhaps it had been more than once; whatever, they'd never talked to her. "I really don't understand why they came out at all. Or what you hope to gain for that matter. Other than boarding some horses out here the last year or so and taking a few lessons, the Cavanaugh woman had nothing to do with us. We've known most of our clients anywhere from five to fifteen years, and I can vouch for all of them."

Not an inch over five feet, with the build of a slight boy, she nonetheless gave the impression of great strength. Ellie could see her whipping a horse around the barrels in a race, a crop stuck between her teeth like the women she'd seen once at a rodeo.

"There's some evidence she was having an affair with someone right before this happened," Ellie said. "Would you have noticed if she seemed particularly attached to anyone out here? Bart, for example, or Rich?"

"Neither of them," the woman said firmly, rocking back on her heels to peer at Ellie. "Bart, well, I wouldn't say he wouldn't have tried, but there's just no way. To put it bluntly, he doesn't have the money to attract someone like her."

She squatted down among her plants and felt around for something. When she located a small plastic marker hidden in the foliage a pleased expression softened her face. "There," she said and jabbed it into the ground. "I have to label them, I've got so many different kinds."

"Then you don't have any idea who it might have been?"

"I haven't the faintest," she replied calmly. With a butter knife she loosened the dirt in a plastic pot and lifted out another plant. "Why don't you go talk to the man who bought her the horses. What was his name, Margolin? He could tell you far more than anyone out here. We barely knew her." She put the plant in the gaping hole she'd dug, eye-balled her next point of entry, and began to dig. "I do get carried away in this garden sometimes. The lady where I buy my plants gets dollar signs in her eyes whenever I drive up with the truck. 'Here's Barbara Norgaard, billfold in hand,' she says, and takes me to the back room where she's put stuff aside for me."

"Your husband mentioned you and he were home the night of the murder," Ellie persisted. "That he watered late and then went to bed. Were you sleeping?"

"No. I was up. He watered around eleven, and we went to bed around twelve. Twelve-thirty maybe. I always wait up for him when he's watering."

"Was Miss Cavanaugh in the habit of coming out in the evenings to ride? After the heat let up a little, I mean?"

"Many of our customers do that in the summer. Either that or come out early in the morning. I couldn't tell you for sure about her. She may have."

"Does your husband have to be over there to help out?"

**65**

"He doesn't have to, but lots of times he'll just do it if he isn't too tired. Someone might need help with a saddle, someone else wants to talk about a horse they have in training. That's why we live out here. Some trainers in the area have houses in town and drive back and forth every day, but it's been a selling point for us that we're always on the premises."

"How long have you owned this place?"

"Fifteen years," she said, gathering up the trowel and the butter knife, tossing them in one of the cardboard flats on the ground by her feet. "We started out in a house trailer over there," she pointed to a spot halfway between the house and the barn, "and after about five years built the house and the pool. The indoor arena we put up about three years ago. If you're from around here you know how cold it gets in the winter."

"How long have you had L'Heureux working for you?"

"Rich," she said with a maternal smile, "is like a son to us. His parents lived in a farmhouse down the road and when they got killed in a car accident back when he was seventeen, we took him in. It's been eight or nine years. He lives on his own now, of course, but we still think of him that way. We never had any kids of our own, you see. We didn't have time, working to make this place go, showing horses all over the country. Not that I regret it. Those were great years. Three days in Texas, then back in the truck and off to Oklahoma. I wish we could take off again like we used to."

"You don't go to the shows anymore?"

She sighed. "Oh yes. I still go off and on. But it's not the same. Nowadays we stick to the tri-state area and have to take anywhere from four to eight clients along. It's not the same."

She squinted up at the sun and then began stacking empty flower pots on the cardboard flats. "Rich's been a big comfort to us and invaluable to Jerry," she said. "Other stables have terrible trouble getting help. Some of them hire illegal immigrants, pay them next to nothing. It's a crime. But we've always been able to count on Rich."

"Do you know if any of your customers had complaints about Miss Cavanaugh? Problems of any sort?"

"Well, Quinn didn't like her," Mrs. Norgaard said calmly. "But I hardly think a thirteen-year-old's dislike is worth mentioning. She claimed the woman was rude to her, treated her like a child. Could be, who knows? But young girls are like that. Decide they don't like someone and that's that. She's a strong-willed little girl not about to put up with anything. And quite a horsewoman for her age. Reminds me of myself when I was younger." Long tail of red hair, Bart had said. Fiery temper to match. There were no signs of that temper now.

Mrs. Norgaard began to pull weeds. She worked quickly and soon there were several sizable piles among the established plants. "Matter of fact, now that we're on the subject, I remember Quinn telling me Bart didn't like her either," she said. "Something about how she thought she was too good for him. But I wouldn't know. I don't pay that much attention to what Quinn says. She's always rattling on, and I just say, 'yes dear, I know what you mean.' And go about my business. Like I told you before, this whole thing has nothing to do with us, and you're wasting your time. The Cavanaugh woman didn't give anyone out here reason to murder her."

Strange way to put it, Ellie thought. No one had said anything about suspecting anyone at the stable of committing the crime . . . She listened absently as Mrs. Norgaard described gardening plans for the following spring: something about creating an oriental garden where weeds now grew. It wouldn't take too much effort, she didn't think. Rich could do the digging for her, and she'd mixed cement before. Perhaps they could even construct a footbridge. Paint it with red enamel . . . or black . . .

Rich L'Heureux was the only one who admitted knowing Sue Anne; everyone else had made it sound like she was an alien in their midst who flitted in and out every day, but no one really knew. Why? Was it a natural aversion to a shocking crime? A clumsy attempt to distance themselves from something they found shocking and unnerving? Or were there other reasons? It was getting late. There would barely be time to run home, shower, and get to the station.

"Mrs. Norgaard," she broke in as the woman paced across the weedy patch counting the feet out loud, "I appreciate you talking to me. I hope I can talk to you again."

Mrs. Norgaard stopped, smiled uncertainly. Clearly she'd assumed she'd never see Ellie again. "Yes, well . . ."

A few minutes later, she watched as Ellie drove down the lane, a perplexed look on her face.

# CHAPTER SEVEN

Ellie could swear she'd seen the tall, thin one in the brown suit, inconspicuous, too inconspicuous, standing on the steps with his hands in his pockets. She craned her neck to see if she could pick out any others. The dark-suited one with the big nose had been planted in the parking lot for quite some time, longer than one would expect even if he was waiting for a tardy family member. Also, the look was subdued but not reverent enough. Had to be, she thought.

She checked her watch. Ten more minutes. How many more people could St. Francis hold and where was Mitch? Probably off somewhere with one of his plainclothes contacts, she thought darkly as she nodded to their cameraman, told him she was going inside.

"Make it tasteful," Fred had said during an earlier meeting of all of them in his office. "And for heaven sakes, don't get close enough to irritate anyone. Use your telephoto lens." People would be touchy at a funeral, and they had to tread cautiously. He hadn't even permitted them to cover the rosary the night before. "I don't care if the other stations use floodlights, we're gonna show some class." The cameraman had nodded.

Mitch had shrugged.

Well, Fred would be proud of them, Ellie thought as she

exchanged stares with the thin, brown-suited man. The camera man had been the soul of discretion, positioning himself so far back while filming that no one had seemed to notice him at all. And she'd stayed with him.

Sue Anne's family had been first to arrive. Mrs. Cavanaugh had been difficult to make out, dressed in black, her face shrouded by a black net. But Mr. Cavanaugh had been just as she'd pictured him after a short telephone conversation earlier in the day. "We don't have anything to tell you people," he'd said curtly then. "We've spoken to the police, and I see no reason to rehash anything with you now." He had a military bearing, closely cropped gray hair, steely blue eyes. He was having a hard time with this, Ellie thought as he herded his enormous brood into the church. In addition to the shock of having his youngest child murdered, he was no doubt anguishing over the media coverage. What father would appreciate a daughter's living arrangements broadcast on television for neighbors and friends to hear about?

Next on the scene had been Shirley Nardo. All bones, with dark circles under her eyes and ratty, dirty-looking hair hanging down her back, she looked as if a strong breeze would blow her away. Phoebe would have been shocked. Heavy into drugs, Ellie concluded, really heavy into drugs.

The Norgaards followed soon after. They had pulled up in a late-model sedan, and Ellie might not have known Jerry Norgaard if he hadn't been with his wife. He was ill-at-ease in his suit, continually tugging at his sleeves, adjusting his tie, while she looked proper in a tailored dress, her hair hidden under a large hat. Why had they come, she wondered. They were joined by Rich L'Heureux a few minutes later, casually dressed in slacks and a white shirt.

And then the man she was waiting for. Ellie told the cameraman to let it roll when a red Porsche squealed into the parking lot and Howard Margolin got out, drawing shocked stares from those mourners who had not yet entered the church. Garbed in an expensive black suit, his dark hair slicked back from a heavily-jowled, flushed face, he had deflected their stares, a deep frown on his face. The cameraman zoomed in and filmed him until he disappeared through the heavy doors. So this had been Sue Anne's boyfriend, the man old enough to be her father, the number one suspect . . . She'd have given anything to catch the expression on Mr. Cavanaugh's face as she spied the man taking a seat at his daughter's funeral.

The young girl, Quinn Farrell, had arrived with her father and mother. It was funny how these horse people looked so out of character in dressy clothing, Ellie thought, taking in Quinn's frilly dress. Especially the horse trainer and this girl. Out of their jeans and boots, they looked uncomfortable, as if their clothes irritated them.

Margaret Simpson had arrived with the doorman, Ed Molina, and a heavy middle-aged woman who was probably his wife.

No Mr. Olson, which didn't surprise her. No Bart Vogel either, she thought now, nodding at the thin, brown-suited man.

"There'll be four or five plainclothesmen watching the crowd," Mitch had pronounced on the drive over, "hoping the murderer just couldn't stay away. This fellow was one of them, Ellie thought, wondering if he'd seen anything he considered suspicious. Had Det. Bieterman sent him to watch anyone in particular? Were the police filming all this from some hidden perch, too?

"What's up?" Mitch asked suddenly at her side.

"It's about to start," she said. "I'm going in."

"Suit yourself."

She went in. A few empty spaces remained in the back, and she sat down just as the organ began to peal.

The copper-colored casket was barely visible through the crowd, but the priest had all eyes on him at the elevated altar. He began with a prayer and followed that with a reading.

What did the two altar boys think, Ellie wondered, as the youngsters, heads bowed differentially, went about their tasks. Had they served at a funeral for someone murdered before? She doubted it.

Ellie studied the backs of the mourners' heads and tried to estimate how many people were there. Plenty. More, she suspected, than would have bothered if the girl had died in a conventional way. Even Phoebe had considered coming, only hadn't because she couldn't arrange a sitter. "Wouldn't you know it," she'd said. "Mother would have to be out of town when I need her . . . "

Ellie didn't think anyone looked familiar, as if they'd gone to Central with her or her sister. Of course, viewing the backs of people's heads wasn't the best angle in which to judge.

Ellie tuned in to the priest again and thought she caught Sue Anne's name. She hadn't known exactly what to expect at a Catholic funeral, but she was a little surprised at the ritualistic nature of the ceremony. Euphemistic, that better described it. No mention of the brutal manner in which she'd died, nothing very personal. Was this typical or was the priest merely being kind to the family?

Ellie shook her head ruefully. If she had to go in such a way, she wanted waving fists, loud outbursts. No such civility.

And then it was over, the procession passing down the center aisle as everyone watched, some pressing tissues to their eyes. First the priest with bells ringing and incense wafting around him, then the casket borne aloft by six husky brothers and brothers-in-law. Ellie knew Mitch was expecting her; she'd promised to meet him out front before the service was over; but she couldn't leave without appearing rude so she sat, watching as those in front of her exited.

"What the hell took you so long?" he asked when she finally joined him on the corner. He was standing by the cameraman as he taped the limousines gliding by, and she ignored his scowl.

"I got hung up."

The drive to the Mt. Pleasant Cemetery was frosty, and Ellie began to wonder if their partnership would last until the case was solved.

Mitch selected a spot slightly below and out of hearing range of the striped canopy where the family and friends stood around the gleaming casket, and, feet planted firmly, began his stand-up while the cameraman filmed it.

"Over two hundred family members and friends made up the funeral procession that is gathered here today to pay their last respects to Sue Anne Cavanaugh. Miss Cavanaugh, the victim of a crime police are working hard to solve and saying little about, will be laid to rest in these peaceful surroundings this afternoon. It is unlikely the scene at police headquarters will be this tranquil for some time . . ." Ellie watched Mrs. Cavanaugh as she laid a rose on the gleaming casket as the cameraman panned slowly across the crowd. Pretty soon it was over and the three of them stood quietly as the crowds streamed toward their cars.

"Let's get back to the air conditioning, shall we?" Mitch suggested. It wasn't until she had stowed her bag in the back seat of the car, was straightening up to get in front, that she noticed the detective some fifty yards away getting into an unmarked car. So he'd been there all along. Wanted to see for himself. Ellie thought about waving but didn't.

Ellie studied Jerry Norgaard's somber face caught in a freeze frame with his wife. She asked the editor to back up the unedited tape, watched Howard Margolin's entrance for the third time, told him to stop the frame just before Margolin turned his back to the camera. There was a hint of cruelty, a suggestion of heavy drinking in the florid complexion, and she stared, fascinated. There was something sensual, too. Were Det. Bieterman and his men giving Margolin a hard time, she wondered, as Mitch told her the police usually did, leaning on their prime suspect to see if he'd break? Or was this his normal reaction to grief? Anger at whomever had murdered his girlfriend.

She heard someone approaching down the hall and in came Mitch.

"Ok. Here's what I want you to do," Mitch said to the editor as he took a seat by him, all business. Quickly, he outlined what he had for an audio track, what sound bites he wanted, and what he thought ought to be included in the video.

The editor asked a couple of questions, an irritated frown developing on his face. He no doubt liked to be given a little license putting the thing together. But Mitch was oblivious. Although the story was fairly routine—reporters covered funerals all the time—Ellie had to admit she was impressed with Mitch's expertise. While he couldn't get too creative with the material, he had a knack for knowing which footage would get the most emotional impact without getting maudlin, and which footage told the story.

After he was finally done, he left, and she and the exasperated editor were alone.

She hated to do it but she asked the editor to show her the tape one more time, and after a sigh and a pointed look at his watch, the guy complied. Of particular interest to her was the scene of everyone clustered together under the canopy at the cemetery. Mr. Cavanaugh, judging by the expression on his face, plainly resented Howard Margolin's presence; he

74

glowered at the other man from time to time though he said nothing. Someone must have pointed Margolin out to him, Ellie thought. At the funeral or during the long climb up the hill to the gravesite.

Shirley Nardo was open in her contempt, too. Not only did she give him hateful looks, but it appeared she muttered something to him as everyone turned to leave. The Norgaards and L'Heureux had heard it by the looks on their faces. She made a mental note to ask Shirley what she'd said.

She thanked the editor and went out.

The newsroom was quiet, Barkley Houston, the city hall reporter, conferring about something with Burrows in his office; always late Winston Davis, the weatherman, already in the studio with Ted Hammond and the sportscaster, waiting for five o'clock and the news.

But at 4:50, word came in of a grain elevator explosion in Andersonville, forty miles west of the city. According to the report, an undetermined number of people were missing and four grain silos and an office building had been flattened in the blast.

"You and you," Fred Burrows said, pointing at Mitch and Barkley Houston, "Take a couple of photographers with you. And you," he said to Ellie, ignoring her hopeful look, "you'll have to cover the city council meeting tonight. Thank God this didn't happen after five. Where the hell is Fenton when I need him?" And he strode out of the newsroom in search of the engineer.

Ellie watched as the four reporters peeled out of the parking lot and tried to console herself. At least she got the council meeting. It beat covering a child-care facility opening or a fireworks disposal demonstration.

Mitch phoned at 6:15 to report that six people were missing, and while another reporter quickly wrote copy to hand to Ted Hammond, currently on the air, Fred Burrows took the receiver and the two men discussed the possibility of going live on the site during their regular evening newscast at ten.

"Investigators say it could be days before they determine the cause of the explosions that killed up to six workers and reduced a grain elevator complex to rubble," Hammond read as Ellie watched on the monitor up on the wall. "The cause is still undetermined, Andersonville Fire Chief George Plank said of the blasts this afternoon at the Fillmore Granary on the banks of the Missouri River."

A city council meeting. Ellie shook her head.

Nobody noticed when she and the photographer left. After hamburgers at a fast-food spot down the street from the station, they drove downtown, parked, and trudged into the city-council chambers. The chief topic on the agenda would be a debate on a rezoning issue, she knew . . .

Where was all the bickering, the cat-calling she'd hoped for, she wondered a short time later. Everything was so business-like, so calm, so sedate. She watched as the cameraman maneuvered the camera back and forth from one bespectacled council man to another and tried not to yawn.

Fred Burrows was still in his office when she got back at nine-thirty.

"What's the latest on Andersonville?"

He tossed down his pencil and looked up at her. "Five still missing. One guy had left work early. Lucky bastard, huh? We go live at ten. How was the council meeting?"

Ellie made a noncommittal noise.

"I want you to go home at midnight," he said. "You look terrible. How much have you slept in the last couple of days?"

Ellie made another noncommittal noise but when midnight came followed his instructions. Only she didn't go directly home. Instead she stopped off at Branigans, a hangout for news people and off-duty nurses and med-techs just down the street from the station. Most nights the two groups intermingled, the hospital crews swapping stories with the journalists. Only tonight was different. It seemed that the news people were too busy congratulating one another on their coverage of the elevator explosion, that and complaining about who did what they didn't like.

"What'd you think of that aerial shot we bagged from the cherry picker?" a reporter from Channel 9 asked Barkley Houston.

"Nice. But I'm scared of heights."

Ellie shouldered her way past the two and ordered a beer at the bar. The guy from the *Sentinel* she kept seeing on the Cavanaugh story—what was his name again, Hancock?—was over in the corner blasting away at a target in some video game, and she made her way in his direction. She'd been meaning to talk to him: he hadn't been with the paper long, newspaper hierarchies weren't all that different from television stations, and she wondered if he was suffering from the same treatment she was getting.

"I'm not complaining," he said simply after he finished nuking a third world terrorist in his game and followed her to a table nearby. Of average height and stocky, he had a prematurely receding hairline and ruddy cheeks, and he reminded her a little of a Nordic pirate, only without the patch and with a good-natured sparkle in his eye.

"I interned at the *Tribune* after I graduated from Minnesota, and when my time there ran out, a friend got me on here. I'm just glad to have a job, any job. It's hard to break into print."

Ellie eyed him intently. "How'd you happen to get the Cavanaugh story then?"

"The murder out at Lakeshore? I work the late shift. Story came in, I went out. I'm not on it anymore. Everything's happening dayside. But I tagged along on that first police briefing out of curiosity. Guy I went along with knew the boyfriend, worked for him once. Small town, this is, for all the people who live here if you know what I mean. Ever wonder what the odds are of a newspaper reporter knowing the prime suspect in a murder investigation he's covering?"

Not all that small, Ellie thought, when you considered a television reporter knew the victim. "What did he say? Your friend. About Howard Margolin. Did he know anything good?"

Hancock set his mug back in the ring of water on the table with a plop. "He was a waiter or a bartender or something at Margolin's lounge back when he was in school. Bob Star? All he said was Margolin was one of those rags-to-riches guys. Grew up in an ethnic neighborhood downtown, dropped out of high school, got married, ran numbers for a while, took his cash, plunked it down on a restaurant, and made it big. Oh, and Bob thought he was a good boss. Said the man was generous as hell, would do anything for a friend. He was going through a divorce while Bob was there, and I guess the wife made out like a bandit when they split up—because he wanted her to." Hancock helped himself to a handful of popcorn and followed that with a mouthful of beer. "His main problem was he couldn't resist women. The marriage broke up because he was messing around with some waitress Bob worked with."

"Whatever happened to her?"

"Lord, I don't know. This was a while back. From the way Bob talked, it wasn't serious. Margolin set up more than one woman in an apartment, gave her a car, jewelry, the works, while he was working there."

"And then what happened'?"

"And then either they got tired of him or vice versa. Probably the latter. My guess is he just quit paying the rent."

Ellie wondered if Sue Anne's affair with Margolin was

headed in that direction. Maybe Margolin had made up the story about her affair with Mr. X in order to drum up a reason to get rid of her. Maybe no Mr. X existed at all; it was just the cruel trick of a man who wanted to dump his gold-digger girlfriend for someone else. But why would he have murdered her? As Hancock pointed out, Margolin held all the cards, all he had to do was quit paying the rent. Unless. Blackmail? Ellie shook her head. Margaret Simpson had heard the two fighting about another boyfriend; she'd pursue that a while longer before drifting into deep waters.

One of the television technicians at a corner table stuck a quarter in the jukebox and strains from an old Beatles tune blared, adding to the already tumultuous din.

Hancock reminded her a little of her boyfriend Gordon, Ellie thought, watching under half-closed lids as he crammed another handful of popcorn into his mouth. Same passivity, same easy-going nature. Only Gordon was in New York where she'd encouraged him to go, and he wasn't writing or calling. There was some graduate assistant he'd mentioned when he'd first arrived there. What had her name been? Tonya? Sonya?

"She's been great, helping me find an apartment, helping me get organized. She's doing her thesis on Chomsky, too," Gordon had told her wonderingly. Chomsky was some linguistic hero to Gordon, in New York to garner his Ph.D. in linguistics. What Chomsky had done she hadn't the faintest idea. What she'd done she was beginning to wonder.

"You've got to go," she'd told Gordon. "You can't pass up such an opportunity; it's a great school. And when I get some experience here, I'll come out. It'll be ideal with you already there."

When Gordon had wavered, not convinced, she'd gotten impatient. "What? You're going to spend your life stuck at the state university? I don't believe it. You have the opportunity to establish solid credentials that will take you wherever you want to go, and you're thinking of staying here? What's wrong with you?" Her arguments had shamed him. He went. Now here she sat. Ellie shook her head.

Hancock said something.

"What's that?"

"I said, care for another beer? I'm buying."

Ellie deliberated. She was so fatigued the only right, the only sensible thing to do was to go home and go to bed. She'd be worthless in the morning if she didn't, and Burrows could take her off the case if he found out she was disobeying his directives, sitting in bars drinking when he'd let her off early so she could rest. On the other hand . . .

"Why not? Make it a light." Twenty minutes, give-or-take wasn't going to kill her, she thought, smiling faintly at Hancock.

# CHAPTER EIGHT

"So Martin says to me, Terry where were you, and I say to him, none of your business, and all the while I'm frantic cause this guy is calling me on the phone, and I'm afraid Martin's gonna pick it up and . . ."

With a perfectly steady hand, the manicurist painted another half moon on the woman's chartreuse nails. She nodded at the appropriate times, smiled, even made sympathetic noises, but she was not listening. At least Ellie got the impression she was not.

Ellie dropped the dog-eared copy of *People* magazine back on the pile of magazines in front of her and shifted in the mauve director's chair. It looked comfortable, but it wasn't. How much longer was it going to take to put the finishing touches on those long spikes, she wondered, catching the manicurist's eye.

"So then . . ." the over-permed blond, her nails splayed out on the table between them, continued, "he said to me, Terry, he said . . ." The manicurist's eyes dropped.

"There must be someone Sue Anne confided in if she had an affair going on the side," she had told Phoebe that morning on the phone while she drank three cups of strong black coffee and tried to wake up. She couldn't have been that discreet or that much of a loner. But who had she told? Shirley Nardo denied knowing about her comings and goings since she had taken up with Howard Margolin, her family was clearly out of the question, and no one at the stable would admit to knowing about her private affairs. So who was left?

It had been something Phoebe said that gave her the idea.

Something about how she had saved over thirty dollars by having a neighbor foil her hair, you just bought one of these little kits at the pharmacy, pulled little swatches of hair through this plastic cap, put on this chemical that stripped the color out and there you were, a fifth of the cost and as professional a job as any hairstylist she'd ever been to had done. But by then Ellie was no longer listening. Her computer was on, and she had started a list. A girl who rode horses day in and day out did not have inch-and-a-half long nails that were real. And she didn't inset diamond chips by herself . . . Armed with a list, she was off shortly after that.

The day was cloudy and hot, and the women in the first two salons she stopped in didn't know Sue Anne Cavanaugh. That didn't stop them from trying to make a sale: perhaps she would like to do something about those chewed nails of hers? But the young woman at the third salon, Exclusively Nails, a shop with striped awnings on Sycamore Street currently promoting a special on Zircon insets according to the sign in the window, did.

"Sue Anne Cavanaugh?" she'd said with a show of interest, "Sure, she came in here. She'd suggested Ellie take a seat, wait until she'd finished with her present customer, the over-permed blond.

Ellie glanced up again. The manicurist was now in the process of writing up a ticket while the customer said something about coming back the following week. Ellie sat up attentively, hoping the woman wouldn't linger long. She got her wish. The woman giggled about something, shot her a curious look and left, letting the door slam behind her.

Now it was Ellie's turn.

"So sad about Sue Anne," the girl said. She had a perfectly round face, foiled, moussed hair, and the most spectacular nails Ellie had ever seen—blood red with lightning bolt strokes in egg-shell yellow and green running horizontally across them—and Ellie took her eyes off them reluctantly.

"Have the police been by?"

No, the manicurist said. But she expected they would. Didn't they eventually get around to talking to everyone?

Ellie nodded, suggested they sit in the waiting area and the girl, Sylvia, she said her name was, said that would be fine; she owned the shop and she could sit where and when she wanted and the waiting area was more comfortable anyway.

She had a glassy-eyed look about her that made Ellie wonder if she'd been smoking something.

"I'm booked solid today," she said, "so we'll have to make this fast. The place has been busy ever since I opened up six months ago. Patrick, he's my boyfriend, he says it's all a matter of timing. You get a decent idea, you have the know-how, and all you need is a little timing. And money of course. I used to do hair, but God that's awful on your feet. Soon as I had a nest egg, I started this place. At least now I get to sit." During this recitation she scooped up a chrome ashtray and took a seat on the small, flowered couch, leaving Ellie the director's chair. She was eyeing Ellie's hair.

"You do your own?" As Ellie nodded, smoothing her long, dark, frizzy hair back, she shook her head. "I can always tell. You know, you ought to try a straightener, or maybe go shorter, emphasize your eyes a little."

They always did that. Every time she went into a beauty salon, someone made some suggestion about her hair, or her makeup, or her nails. Ellie closed her eyes. It wasn't the fact

**83**

that they said anything that was so irritating—it was second nature to them to want to guide someone into a chair and go to it, it was their daily bread. But why did she always have to pretend it didn't annoy her to death? She could care less.

"Tell me about Sue Anne Cavanaugh," she said. "Did she come in often?"

Once a week, Sylvia replied promptly, sometimes more often depending on what she was up to. If she was going out somewhere fancy she had to have them on, if she was going to a horse show, she had to have them off. "Nails, I mean. She was always breaking them and then running in here for a patch-up job. I'd have to say she was one of my best customers."

Money. She had had plenty of that. And she hadn't been afraid to spend it. "You need those kinds of customers to make it, you know," she said matter-of-factly. Often Sue Anne wanted insets—Sylvia started up to get a tray of them, try to talk Ellie into a Zircon perhaps?—but Ellie waved her back to her seat, that wasn't necessary. One or two times Sue Anne had even given them back to her after wearing them to some function or another, she continued, which was unheard of. "They aren't exactly cheap, you know."

"She was quite generous then?"

"Oh yes. She was great." The manicurist pulled out a cigarette and a lighter that matched her fingernails, identical lightning bolts on a blood-red background. "Like that?" She held out the lighter. "That's where I got the idea for the nails." She waved her fingers coquettishly. "You wouldn't believe where you find designs. Sue Anne always liked my ideas. She'd try anything once." She lit her cigarette, inhaled deeply. Apparently the law about smoking didn't apply in her own shop.

"Did you two talk while you worked?"

Sylvia nodded. "Sure. What was the guy's name? The

boyfriend?"

"Howard Margolin."

"Yeah. Howie, she called him. No, wait, old man. She usually called him the old man. We talked about him." She smiled, ashed her cigarette in the big chrome bowl on her lap. "She used to make jokes about him. Said he couldn't keep up with her, he was in a little over his head with her. She said he almost had a heart attack one time after, well, you know . . ." She looked a little embarrassed. "Well, anyway, yeah we talked."

"Did you get the impression he was good to her? That they got along pretty well?"

She nodded. "She had him wrapped around her little finger to hear her talk. I mean, I don't know if I'd want to be in her situation, exactly, you know, living with somebody who could be my father, hell, my grandfather, but the money was great, she always said. The trips she took, the clothes he bought her." She glanced around the salon a little uncertainly. "Sometimes I think it wouldn't be half bad, not having to work your ass off day in and day out like I have to. 'Course," she added, squaring her shoulders, "Patrick says if I play my cards right, six months from now I'll be able to hire other girls to do the work, and I can sit back and rake it all in."

Ellie wondered idly what Patrick did for a living and how much of the girl's money he planned to rake in. "Did you ever meet Mr. Margolin yourself?"

The girl shook her head.

Ellie brought up the autopsy results, recited the precise amounts of Vicodin, marijuana and alcohol the Medical Examiner had found in Sue Anne's body, and a guarded look settled like a thin veil over the girl's face. She ran her hand through her hair, fluffing the wet-looking curls so they stood up a little, and licked her lips uncertainly.

"I don't know anything about that . . ."

"She never mentioned smoking a little marijuana, taking a few downers?" Ellie made it sound like she was incredulous, everyone had known Sue Anne took drugs.

Well, as a matter-of-fact . . . she had mentioned it once or twice, she said hurriedly. She had done stuff occasionally, she said again, but she was no big user, she was a, oh, what did they call it, a . . . a recreational user—the girl nodded at the recollection—that was it, a recreational user, and she didn't do it often. She blinked, looking ashamed of having made this admission.

"How about where she got the stuff? She ever talk to you about that?"

"Nope."

She was beginning to look sullen, and Ellie let it slide. "Did she mention any other boyfriends? Guys she might have had an interest in?"

"The guy at the stable you mean?"

Ellie shifted almost imperceptibly in her chair. Yes. That was the one. What had his name been . . . ?

"I'm not sure." Sylvia pursed her lips, took another deep drag on her cigarette, flicked an ash off her short skirt. Sue Anne had always been talking about those cowboys at that stable, she explained, how one had said this to her and another had said that. They all had the hots for her, phoned her, wanted to take her out. But there had been this one . . . Sylvia crossed her thin legs, tugged at her skirt. One of them she had actually messed around with. What had his name been? She shrugged.

More than once whoever it was had tried to break it off with Sue Anne, and she'd come in pretty upset about it, saying she'd make life hell for him, he couldn't treat her that way. "But," and here she paused, trying to recall what had generally happened, "next time she'd come in, it was funny. She'd say everything was okay again, she'd calmed him down,

I don't know how, and she'd be happy." Sylvia scratched her head with a long nail, turned her blue eyes on Ellie. "She had a way with guys, you know."

What about Bart Vogel, Ellie asked. Had she ever heard that name? Was he one of the cowboys she talked about?

The girl considered it, mouthing the name slowly, turning it over on her tongue. "Hmmm, I don't think so," she said finally, sounding unsure. "I think she mentioned him once or twice, but he wasn't the one, you know, that she was having this thing with."

Why not? What made her so sure of that?

Because she'd just remembered something that might be helpful in figuring out who that person was, she said matter-of-factly, glancing up at the cheap plastic clock on the wall, suddenly letting out an expletive when she realized how late it was. With a frown she stubbed out her cigarette, twisted around to peer out the window behind her, see if her next client was in sight. She was always late, Mrs. Markel was, she said disgustedly, standing up with a flounce; always brought her kids along though she, Sylvia, had asked her politely not to because the kids destroyed the waiting area every time and she, Mrs. Markel, said nothing, leaving it up to Sylvia to try to keep them in line and at the same time do a halfway decent job on her nails.

"What was it that you remembered?"

Sylvia stopped in the motion of shoving the chrome ashtray on a high shelf above the sofa—those damn kids delighted in playing in the butts, dumping it over when they'd had enough of it— "It was something about . . ." she made an effort to remember. "Oh sure. It was that you could strike most of the cowboys out there," she said. "Figure they weren't the one."

Why was that?

"Because," she said, her face transforming into a relieved

**87**

smile—there was Mrs. Markel now coming up the walk without the two brats— "Because," she repeated, "the guy she had the affair with had a wife. He was worried about his wife. She'd leave him, he kept telling Sylvia, if she found out."

"I suspect the manicurist was doing drugs with Sue Anne," Ellie explained to Phoebe over egg salad sandwiches in her sister's kitchen. There was quite a commotion going on. Her nephew, Brandon, banged on a stainless steel bowl with a spoon, and the baby, Todd, wailed from his swing suspended from the doorframe.

Phoebe gave him a cracker and he stopped for the moment.

"Which was why she wasn't completely open with me. Not to mention I think she was stoned."

"This morning?"

Ellie nodded. The reason for her guilt may have been as insignificant as sharing an occasional joint; whatever, it didn't really matter. "I never would have guessed she and the horse trainer were involved," she said aloud. "Bart Vogel was a bachelor, and so was Rich L'Heureux. By process of elimination that leaves Jerry Norgaard."

He had described Sue Anne as a woman he didn't know well, someone whose personal life he knew nothing about, Ellie recalled. She frowned in concentration, trying to remember anything else he may have said, anything his wife or the hired hand had said.

"Do you think his wife knew? Knows now?" Phoebe set a bowl of grapes on the table, and Ellie broke off a sprig absentmindedly.

"I was just wondering about that. Barbara Norgaard didn't act like it, but then what does that mean. She could be a helluva actress for all I know. What I remember is she was positive the murder had nothing to do with anyone at the stable. Oh, and she seemed exasperated that I was there asking questions."

"Well, what are you going to do now? You can't very well tell her it's come to light that Sue Anne was having an affair with her husband and ask her for the details. How much she knows, when she found out, what she did about it. First off, if she does know, she's already pretended she didn't, and I doubt she's about to confess now. And second, if she doesn't know, you hardly want to put yourself in the position of being that kind of messenger. You could have another murder on your hands."

"I ought to call Det. Bieterman," Ellie said reluctantly.

Todd started to cry again, and Phoebe handed him another cracker. This time it failed to pacify him. "Time for a nap," she said, scooping him up. "You, too, buster," she said to Brandon, still banging on his makeshift drum, a half-eaten sandwich pulverized on its top. With the baby under one arm she cleaned the peanut butter off the other, squirming and fighting—drum, he wanted his drum—while Ellie procrastinated. Should she call him? He never called her. The investigation was in its fourth day, and she had yet to hear anything from him. "He's not in the office," she was told, or "He'll get back to you later," which of course he never did. Did she really owe him anything?

It would be to her advantage, she decided. He was better suited for the sticky task of confronting Jerry Norgaard, who, she was sure, would merely tell her to leave if she tried to question him. And, if she passed on information like this, he'd have to keep her informed of the outcome. She'd insist.

Ellie pulled out her phone. "He's not in right now. Can he get back to you?" the same man who always answered his phone said.

Ellie bit her lip, took a guess. "Det. Morrison? Is that

you?"

"No. This is Wilson."

"Wilson. Tell him it's important, will you? Tell him I have some information for him I think he'll want to hear about."

Wilson took down her name and number and promised the message would be relayed.

"I guess that's all I can do, barring marching up to his office, sitting at his desk," she told Phoebe when she came back.

"You think he'll call?"

"Who knows?"

Phoebe made them some hot tea, and the two of them sat over the steaming mugs, quietly discussing Ellie's next moves while the two young boys napped.

## CHAPTER NINE

The apple pie had tasted mighty fine, he was to recall, and Harlan Linstrom had beamed at his wife in appreciation. She could surely bake. He took another bite of the still warm pastry, savoring it, soon finished the generous wedge and put in an order for seconds, but shook his head, drew the line when Bessie suggested a scoop of strawberry ice cream on the side.

Nope, he was getting fat, he said, rubbing his expanding girth. Two pieces of pie was plenty and besides, his overalls were starting to feel snug. She smiled at that, a heavy woman herself who had always ascribed to the belief that a bountiful crop was to be enjoyed and by who better than the family that produced it. Covering the pie, she resolved to put it out again at suppertime when his defenses would again be weak.

He had some fence down on the south eighty he was going to put right, he said; it was those kids down the road short cutting down to the creek, did it. "Wish their parents'd teach 'em to respect another man's property," he grumbled, though they both knew he didn't really care; having raised four boys of their own on the farm, they knew it was impossible to keep up with them all the time, and boys-would-be-boys.

But a rear tire on his old pickup looked low and whistling

"Chattanooga Choo Choo," he headed out to the highway first, turned east, drove the five miles to Charlie Michael's Texaco station for some air. There he inquired after his pal Charlie; and when Charlie's son, Dan, said he was in having some dental work done, expressed the hope they didn't do to Charlie what they'd done to him, revealing a set of perfect dentures. Dan assured him such was not the case; his father had merely gone to have his teeth cleaned; and with this reassuring news he drove off with a wave, heading back the way he had come.

Mrs. Barnett, their neighbor and mother of the offending boys, was out in her yard hanging a load of sheets on the line; and he waved to her, too, before proceeding down the gravel road to the sagging fence, pulling off to the shoulder, pocketing the key carefully. Didn't want to misplace that.

Closer inspection revealed one post down, tipped on its side like someone had sat on it, and the barbed wire laying in the field close to the cornrows. He got busy, righting the post, tamping the earth down hard around it with a shovel, was just putting on his gloves when he spotted one of the Barnett boys ducking into a cornrow fifty yards down the gravel lane.

"Hey boy, you get outta there," he shouted, and without thinking, took off after the kid. He didn't mind if the boys stayed on the edge of the field passing down to the creek, but he sure didn't want them trampling around in his corn.

But, just as quickly he realized he was too old to be running, especially on such a hot day—Bessie'd kill him if she saw him—and he slowed to a walk. Slowly now he trudged on and a few steps further, he spied the boy's white t-shirt ahead of him, motionless in the heat.

What in tarnation did the boy think he was doing, he asked, as the boy turned his head to look at him—Toby, his name was—pale-looking, like he was sick or something.

Harlan was immediately contrite—he shouldn't have chased him, scared the bejesus out of him, he started to say—but the boy turned away, scarcely paying any attention to him; and, indignation renewed, he marched forward, shoved the green foliage out of his way, reached out a restraining arm. It was then that he spied what had caused that peculiar look on the boy's face.

"There she was, lying there like a sack of bones, right smack dab in the middle of my cornfield," he told Det. Bieterman. "Never thought I'd live to see the day . . ."

That was an apt remark, Bieterman thought now as he gazed down at the stringy hair, the smudges under the closed eyes. She had been dumped, literally, like someone's garbage; she lay on her back, her arms flung over her head, one leg crumbled under her slight frame. Clad in jeans and a white blouse, she still sported a colorful string of Indian beads around her neck, an irony not lost on him since, he was pretty sure, she, too, had been strangled. Someone hadn't wanted her found quickly, he remarked to Morrison. What were the odds of her being found so soon out here in the middle of nowhere.

It was late afternoon, unbearably hot, and he and Morrison trudged back through the trampled cornrow, leaving the forensics guys and the photographer room to do their jobs. He had recognized her at once, and he worried now that Lieutenant Borden would throw more men into the investigation.

A crowd of neighbors, reporters and cameramen greeted them when they emerged from the hedgerows. Pressed forward expectantly, restrained only by a flimsy crime scene ribbon tacked hastily to Linstrom's broken down fence, they were clearly anxious for news.

Ellie Schimmel and that pain Mitch Bassman were among them, Bieterman saw as he stepped forward to make his statement.

He made it short; gave them the sex and probable age of the victim, indicated there were suggestions of foul play, and told them they would have to wait for definite cause and time of death until the Medical Examiner reported that information to him. A flurry of questions broke out—Had they identified the woman? Was she strangled like the other one? Were there connections between the two cases?—but he held up his hand for silence, told them he'd released all the information he could for the time being, and reminded them not to enter the crime scene area until the body had been removed and the physical search completed.

Before he'd reached his car, snaking his way through the snarl of emergency vehicles, patrol cars, and sheriff cruisers, the reporters had turned to the farmer, Linstrom, who'd found the body, and were firing questions at him; taping the bespectacled old man's replies while he gesticulated, frowned, pointed toward the fence, finally took off his hat revealing a shiny bald head.

"You got out of that one easy enough," Morrison said admiringly, starting his engine while Bieterman calculated the best way to bypass the clogged road—if they headed south, followed the bend barely visible through the cornfields ahead, they'd hit Highway 97, and that would take them back to the main road— "I said, you pulled yourself away from that pretty fast," Morrison repeated.

Bieterman grunted. "Go left," he said, then glanced in the side mirror. The crowd shrank as the sergeant stepped on the gas, maneuvered around the last car and took off.

"I mean, they'd be fence posts not to suspect a connection," he continued, "but at least we got a couple hours jump on 'em before they have it confirmed."

Bieterman grunted again. The press and what they did or didn't know did not concern him nearly as much as find-

94

ing out how Captain Borden would react to the news. If he could convince him not to clutter up the case with too many chiefs, he, Bieterman, could get on with the job, could map out a clear course of strategy for finding the perpetrator.

"Think that female reporter, you know, the one you talked to the other day, figured out who the victim is?" Morrison wondered.

"I don't know," he said thoughtfully. "Depends on what kind of a description she wrings out of that farmer, I suppose." Ellie Schimmel, it occurred to him, was the one who'd dropped the slain woman's name, initiating an interview between the woman and himself only the day before. Had it not been for her, he wouldn't have been able to make the instant identification he had just made at the scene; in addition, it could have taken some time to confirm the connection between the two murders. He'd been regretting the fact he'd talked to her that day in his office, especially when he saw the messages that had stacked up on his desk from her in the past few days; but now he began to wonder if he'd made a tactical error in avoiding her, if it hadn't actually been a good thing they'd conferred.

Morrison drew up to the stop sign, waited while a semi whizzed by, then turned right onto the highway back toward town. "Well," he said with a frown, "she'll know soon enough, won't she. They'll all know soon enough. And then we're going to have our hands full."

# CHAPTER 10

" . . . Admitting only that there are what they call similarities in the two cases, local police are refusing to speculate tonight on the possibility that both women were murdered by the same person."

The phone rang for Ellie.

"Tell whoever it is to hold, will you?" Ellie frowned as Mitch continued his delivery on the television monitor.

"Area farmer Harlan Linstrom first notified sheriff deputies around two p.m. after he and a neighboring youth stumbled across the body in his cornfield." The video cut to Linstrom, looking shaken as he pointed toward the field and recounted his story about the broken fence and his pursuit of the young boy. Then back to Mitch. "Metropolitan police admit tonight an interview with the slain woman was conducted only yesterday afternoon but will not say what that interview concerned. Reporters have determined that the women were close friends; that they had, for several years after high school graduation, shared an apartment on Glebe Road." Reporters, Ellie sniffed. She had supplied the information, no one else. Not to mention the name. Had she not known, figured out who the victim was, long before Bieterman confirmed it at his evening press briefing, they could not have had two tapes readied for airtime: a benign one with scant information, and the one she was now viewing. Bieterman waited on purpose, she thought now, knowing it would wreak havoc in the newsrooms.

The camera angle widened to include police headquarters behind him as Mitch wrapped it up. " . . . While family members make funeral arrangements and wonder how and why their daughter and sister was murdered, police will say only that they are not without leads and that they are working hard to solve this latest slaying, the second in less than a week." There were a few seconds of silence and then, looking stern, "This is Mitch Bassman, reporting for WBTV."

Ellie shook her head. Kudos from Fred Burrows were unlikely, she knew, unless she blew her own horn. Suddenly she remembered the call waiting for her and picked up the receiver.

It was Det. Bieterman sounding polite but tired. She had something that might be of importance to the investigation?

Ellie's first impulse was to hang up on him, the Cavanaugh investigation be damned. She was holding her own, scoring points without him, and he wasn't that much help when they were communicating. Not to mention the fact that conducting a press briefing thirty minutes before airtime was infuriating. But then common sense prevailed. That and curiosity.

"You must be pretty busy over there right now," she said. "Especially with this second murder."

He was, he agreed. "But I'd like to go over everything you can remember from your conversation with Miss Nardo. You've already told me about it, of course, but I want to get it down for the record. And find out what it was you called me about."

Ellie paused, not sure if it was in her best interest to tell him why she'd called. Would she get anything out of it? She sighed. At this point, she guessed she'd just have to hope so. "I talked to Sue Anne Cavanaugh's manicurist," she said slowly, and then outlined the gist of her conversation with the manicurist, told him Sue Anne had been having an affair with a married cowboy from the stable. Norgaard, of course.

He'd look into it, he said sounding guarded. First thing in the morning.

"And will I hear the results of that interview?"

There was silence at the other end. He cleared his throat. "You know the diner opposite my office? I'll meet you there around noon. You can tell me about Shirley Nardo, and I'll tell you what I find out."

Ellie smiled.

"I don't know what I'll get out of him," she admitted to Tom Hancock later at Branigans, "but at least he realizes he's not in for a free ride."

The bar was crowded as usual, and finding Hancock blasting away again at his video game, she'd coerced him into sitting at a corner table by promising him a beer.

"You know, I don't understand why he agreed to talk to me the day of the first press briefing and then clammed up."

"Probably had second thoughts." Tom drew a line down the moisture on his glass, dividing the container into two even halves, then added some curlicues and dots. "Happens all the time. You have to be careful who you tell what to when you're in a position like he is."

Ellie supposed he was right, though she still resented it. She leaned back in her chair. "Shirley Nardo knew something," she said, turning to the second murder. "Either she saw or heard something that made her dangerous, I'm guessing. And if it wasn't so pat, I'd say Margolin did it. You know, murdered Sue Anne out of rage, then killed her friend after she accused him of it. But it's too simple, too obvious. It just couldn't have happened that way."

Tom looked thoughtful. "You said she was heavy into drugs. Maybe she tried to blackmail Margolin because she was desperate for money."

Ellie shook her head. No matter how big a mess the girl was, she didn't believe she'd stoop to that. "Sue Anne was her best friend, remember?"

Tom nodded. "But you said she was jealous of Sue Anne. They were no longer close friends."

"I don't buy it. She may have been jealous, but she didn't hate her." Ellie took a sip of her beer. "You know, it occurred to me when I was reading through my notes from the day I went out to the Norgaard Stable, Shirley hadn't ever been out there. She didn't even know the name of it when I asked."

"Meaning?"

"Meaning she never met any of those people, the Norgaards, Vogel, L'Heureux, any of them. At least not through Sue Anne."

Hancock looked unperturbed. "So?"

"Don't you see? If one of them had anything to do with murdering Sue Anne, and there are motives, what motive could there have been to kill someone no one knew? At least as far as I know."

"Drugs," Hancock guessed. "She sold one of them some Vicodin or marijuana. That's how whoever did it made the connection, knew the two girls were friends."

Ellie shrugged. "Maybe," she said. Privately she thought it sounded too coincidental. She'd talk to Shirley's mother, she decided; see what, if anything, Mrs. Nardo could tell her about her daughter's comings and goings, her friends and acquaintances.

"How's your work?" she asked Hancock when he returned with another round of beers.

"They're treating me decent. Look at tomorrow's paper. I got a front-page story about the murder with a good jump, page three, I think. At least it's not buried in the back."

"How'd you manage that?"

"Simple. Stuff broke after the big shots went home. Bieterman times his announcements for my benefit, I think. You know, I ought to thank him, get into his good graces like you have. Maybe I'll end up dayside." He grinned good-humoredly, and Ellie was reminded of Gordon again.

"Hey, I was only kidding. What's the matter? You look like you're afraid I'll steal your lollipop."

That had already been stolen, Ellie thought, forcing herself to smile. You couldn't steal what apparently had already been stolen.

# CHAPTER ELEVEN

Det. Bieterman stretched, took a large gulp of coffee, and pushed away from his desk. It was dark outside, patrol cars gleamed below him, and his eyes wandered slowly up past the faint skyline to the moon, shining palely through a humid cloud cover. It was at its peak, a huge round sphere low on the horizon; and as he watched it, letting his mind go blank, some of the tension that had built up during the long day eased out of his shoulders and neck. The phone rang, and he reached for it almost languidly.

It was Det. Morrison calling to say they'd located the girl's car in the old warehouse district between Barker and Cleveland, and they'd check out the local bars and diners in the morning. After a few terse suggestions, the detective replaced the receiver and drank more coffee. The lab would go over the car with a fine-tooth comb, he knew, but somehow he doubted they'd turn up much.

The Medical Examiner had phoned with confirmation the girl had been strangled like her friend, the jargon sounding like a carbon copy of the Cavanaugh girl's autopsy report. The difference this time was that the young woman had been awake and there'd been a struggle. Contusions on her legs suggested she'd been surprised from behind and had inflicted most of the bruises to herself as she kicked wildly, trying to escape her attacker. Probably in her own car, Bieterman thought dispassionately, wiped clean for their benefit.

He frowned as he recalled his earlier evening movements, searching her apartment, then knocking on neighbors' doors, trying to shake some amnesia out of them. A transient bunch, only a few admitted knowing her and none remembered having seen her around lately.

Bieterman pulled a colored snapshot out of the folder on his desk and peered at it closely. It had begun to lose its color with age and the faces were blurred—it hadn't been a good picture to begin with—but it was of the two young women: Sue Anne grinning drunkenly for the photographer, the Nardo woman, her arm around her friend, looking wild. Bieterman turned the snapshot over. According to the childish-looking scrawl on the back, it was two years old; "Partying Dogs," one of them had titled it. He dropped it back in the folder.

The apartment had been a mess of dirty dishes and beer cans; sifting through it they'd discovered razor blades, syringes, and a bag of cocaine carelessly stuffed in the girl's closet. Forensics had lifted a set of clear prints but Bieterman doubted that would lead to anything. This person was too clever for that.

"She wasn't never home," a teenage boy from the next door apartment had volunteered. Dressed in filthy jeans, no shirt, with a handful of keys secured to his belt by a ring, he ought to have been too young to act so indifferent, Bieterman thought. "I seen a few guys in and out, but I don't know who they was."

The apartment complex had originally been a motel, converted to rental units when no one cared to vacation in that area of town any longer. Bieterman had been glad when it was time to leave.

"I know you're doing everything you can," Cpt. Borden

had said reassuringly when he'd charged into the Homicide Chief's office late that afternoon, prepared to do battle to retain autonomy in the investigation. "Just clear the thing up as fast as you can before the news media people whip everybody into a frenzy over this thing, start scaring everybody with headlines about crazed killers."

Whoever it was was anything but crazed, Bieterman thought, finishing his cup of coffee. God, he needed to go home, get some sleep. He'd have to release the autopsy results in the morning, talk to the horse trainer, meet that reporter for lunch . . . Maybe she'll have solved the thing by then, he thought, beginning to chuckle suddenly. She was tenacious enough. But was that all it took? He slumped back in his chair and thought about that for a while. Enthusiasm only got you so far. You also needed a sixth sense, plenty of endurance and a little luck. Most of the cases he handled proved easy to solve: he and Morrison caught the perpetrator red-handed, witnesses came forward, or the lack of premeditation made their task easy. But cases like this one were baffling. When someone went to the pains this killer had, down to wearing gloves and knowing when the doorman took his breaks, things got tough. That's when he needed to pull out all the stops, use whatever means he could to trap the guilty one.

Like consulting with that reporter. What a hot shot. Bieterman chuckled again. She reminded him a little of himself fifteen years ago, out to climb the ranks, make a name for himself.

Had it been worth it? In his case, he supposed so. Although it hadn't left much time for a personal life. He'd never married, lived alone. He'd had girlfriends, a few over the years, but he wasn't around enough; and when it had finally sunk in that his work was more important to him than any of them, the women had drifted off. The price he'd had to pay, he thought philosophically. The price he still paid.

Det. Morrison poked his head in the door: he was finished for the night and thought he'd head home.

Sounded like a good idea, Bieterman agreed. He closed the file in front of him, stretched again, snapped off the light.

Dett. Morrison was a good guy, he mused as he headed for his car out on the street. He hadn't thought so at first. The father of five, Morrison had been too opinionated, too accustomed to being the boss to accept direction the first year they'd been paired together. Bieterman had been forced to sit on him a few times. But things had worked out; today their relationship was more than a professional liaison. They had become friends. Of course, Morrison deferred to him when protocol demanded, took orders without question when they were called for, but there was an easy camaraderie between them that transcended work. In fact, if he were asked, Bieterman would have to say Morrison was his best friend.

Wonder if Lila Morrison's mad at me tonight, Bieterman thought, looking at his watch. It was one-thirty. He hoped not. Surely the detective's wife understood.

# CHAPTER TWELVE

Twenty-one seventeen Briarcliff, a green stucco that had seen better days, was in a fringe area grown quite shabby. Garbage cans lay on their sides, weeds choked out occasional patches of lawn, and discarded cars, denude of tires, sat in driveways. The house looked like it was being consumed by the climbing roses that grew wild across the sagging front porch, and the pungent scent of rotting blossoms assailed Ellie as she picked her way to the front door and knocked. Mrs. Nardo let her in with a brave smile. She was in her mid-sixties, Ellie guessed, though by her careworn appearance she looked closer to seventy-five. There was a resigned look to her that suggested she had expected bad news like this for a long time and really wasn't too surprised when it actually came.

She shared the small house with her father, she explained when an elderly man peeked around the corner from the kitchen and stared at Ellie with vacant eyes.

"Make yourself a cup of tea, Papa," she suggested listlessly. "He'll burn the place down one of these days," she whispered to Ellie when he had shuffled out of view, "but it gives him something to do, bless his soul. The policemen and you reporters have him all worked up."

Early on, Ellie could see she didn't know much. Mother

and daughter weren't close, she said: Shirley blew in every once in a while to say hello and get a free meal and then she was off again, doing whatever it was she did. "She had a job stuffing little toys in cereal boxes back in March," she said vaguely when Ellie asked about employment. "But I'm not sure where. And for all I know, that job may have ended. Shirley never stayed put too long."

She didn't know or care much about Sue Anne Cavanaugh's activities; the mention of her name only seemed to arouse a half-hearted anger. "That girl," she said, shaking her head, "caused nothing but trouble in this house starting back when the girls were in seventh grade. Traipsing in here all painted up like a you-know-what with her skirts hiked up so you could see everything. My husband and I kept telling Shirley to stay away from her, but she wouldn't listen. I'm sure things would never have come to this if Shirley hadn't ever met Sue Anne." Pressing a tissue to her eyes, she got up and went over to the mantle to adjust the plastic-covered print of the crucifixion hanging above it.

"Shirley's younger brother," Mrs. Nardo said when she was more composed, "thought I should kick Shirley out. Back in high school after their father died, and Shirley was drinking and smoking marijuana, this was. But somehow I couldn't do that, turn my own daughter out on the streets. Who knows, maybe things would have worked out better if I had. She'd have gotten herself hooked up."

She fetched a photograph off the mantel and passed it to Ellie. It was a family portrait of the brother, Andrew, his wife and two boys. Andrew had sergeant's stripes on his sleeves. "He's stationed in Germany now," she said. "Calls me once a month."

"Very handsome," Ellie murmured. Andrew looked nothing like his sister: he was towheaded and clean shaven, looked like an all-American athlete. She passed the photo back to his mother. "Did your daughter ever mention how she felt when Sue Anne moved out?"

"She didn't like·it. She was mad for quite a while. 'That man's sixty-something, Ma,' she told me. 'Sue Anne's out of her mind.' But eventually she calmed down and made do. I told her then it was time to get away from Sue Anne permanently, have nothing more to do with her, but she didn't listen. Sue Anne was like a sister to her, she said." Mrs. Nardo settled uncertainly on the couch and adjusted a bobby-pin in her gray hair.

"She told me a couple of times she didn't like the way Sue Anne was changing, putting on airs over the money and cars and all that man gave her, but Shirley kept in touch with her anyway. Sue Anne would come around someday, she seemed to feel. And who wouldn't get a little stuck on herself the way that man spent money on her, she said. Shirley got to making excuses for her later on, you see."

The kettle screeched out in the kitchen, and they could hear the grandfather's stentorian breathing as he made his way to the stove.

"Would you like a cup? Grandpa probably heated only a thimbleful of water but I could put some more on."

No, Ellie said. She didn't care for any, thank you. "Could you just tell me," she asked, "the names of any friends Shirley saw recently? Did she bring anyone by or mention anyone?"

Mrs. Nardo furrowed her brow. She didn't know any of their names, she said. "But they weren't the kind of people you'd want your daughter hanging around with. Spooks, they were. Why, a few months back one of them stole a silver mug I got as a wedding present from my grandfather. Used to keep it on my whatnot shelf over there." Ellie's attention was directed to a small bookshelf under the west window filled with cheap bric-a-brac she'd collected over the years. "I'm sure he did it while Shirley and I were in the kitchen.

Scooped it up faster than lightning. Those kind have big pockets if you know what I mean. I finally put my foot down with Shirley. No visits unless she was alone."

There was the suggestion that these friends, this one in particular anyway, had a drug problem like Shirley did. As delicately as she could Ellie brought it up. Something to the effect that Shirley had looked as though she might have experimented with more than just marijuana and alcohol.

"Experimented," Mrs. Nardo hooted mirthlessly. "She was an addict. So was he, the one I just told you about who swiped my mug. Probably the one who introduced her to half the poison she got into. Either him or another derelict she ran into after Sue Anne moved out. I have to admit I gave up on her when she got into the cocaine and all. You're never supposed to do that, give up on your own child, but I have to say I did. The devil'd got ahold of her was how I looked at it."

"But you don't recall his name? This one you're talking about?"

"Tommy, maybe. Johnny. Something like that." She shook her head and clucked like a disapproving hen. "Nobody should have to suffer like I have. First I lose my husband, then my daughter."

When was the last time she'd come by, Ellie asked gently.

Indignation and self-pity evaporated at the recollection of their last meeting. "Three weeks ago," she said. "I made her a nice plate of rigatoni and sausage, we talked a while, and she left. Who'd have thought it would be the last time I'd see her?"

Could she remember what they'd talked about?

It was nothing much that stuck in her mind, Mrs. Nardo replied. They'd discussed her new apartment, how she liked it, that sort of thing. "She looked like she hadn't had a square meal in weeks, but she said everything was okay, she was eating normally. You know, you couldn't nag at the girl too much or she wouldn't come around at all . . ." Mrs. Nardo's voice trailed off.

"Did she mention Sue Anne? Or this Tommy?"

Mrs. Nardo nodded. "She said the young man had helped her move her stuff. And she talked about some parties she'd been to with him. But she didn't mention Sue Anne. 'Least not that I recall."

There was the sound of something shattering in the kitchen and Mrs. Nardo rose resignedly. "Grandpa's broken another cup, I imagine. Excuse me."

Ellie heard her murmur something to the old man, the sound of a cupboard door opening and closing, the swishing of a broom. Ellie's eyes strayed to the Bible, open on the table in front of her. ". . . be warned . . . Serve the Lord with fear, with trembling kiss his feet, lest he be angry, and you perish in the way; for his wrath is quickly kindled. Blessed are all who take refuge in him . . ."

"My only consolation, that," Mrs. Nardo said, back again on silent feet. "That and Andrew. Though Andrew," she said, adjusting the bobby pin in her stringy hair again, "isn't coming to the funeral. It's hard to make ends meet on a sergeant's pay, he says. Living in a foreign country like Germany isn't cheap, and supporting a wife and two children is harder there than here, he tells me. Still, I wish he could come. He told me I ought to come over there sometime. Where am I going to get the money to do that?"

The army made provisions under these circumstances, Ellie said. "I had a second-cousin whose father died, and the government sent him back and picked up the tab. I'm sure they'd do the same for your son."

Mrs. Nardo smiled and blew her nose. "Are you sure? Andrew didn't mention anything like that."

"Call him up. Tell him to discuss it with his commander. Like I said, my cousin was taken care of."

She would, Mrs. Nardo said, smiling even wider. She'd do just that. In better spirits, she held the family photograph out again for Ellie to admire, provided the grandsons' names, their ages, their grades in school.

It was a mistake saying anything about Andrew's entitlements, it struck Ellie as she crossed the sagging front porch later. Andrew was a sergeant, presumably a career officer in the United States Army. Anyone who worked for the U.S. government, in whatever capacity, knew the benefits before signing up. And if he wasn't aware of this one, no doubt his commander had told him by now. He didn't want to come. His sister's death didn't occasion the grief one normally expected in a sibling.

Ellie picked up the plastic menu, ran her eyes down the poorly typed list, and decided on a cheeseburger. When the waitress had taken their orders and moved off to the next table, she brought up the question foremost in her mind—whether he'd been out to the stable yet.

Det. Bieterman dumped a packet of sugar in his coffee, added cream and stirred thoughtfully before he finally answered. "Early this morning. And your information was correct." The Norgaard and Cavanaugh affair had begun at a horse show, he said, while Ellie congratulated herself. Jerry Norgaard had admitted going to bed with the woman in her motel room during a two-day event in Salina, Kansas. He shrugged.

Ellie tried to picture the upright, moralistic horse trainer sneaking around a motel, paying nocturnal visits to Sue Anne Cavanaugh. "Did they only meet at the shows? Never at her apartment?"

"After the one time in Salina, Norgaard said they agreed they'd been too indiscreet, and they switched to meeting at her apartment."

"Wasn't he afraid of running into Margolin there?"

"He said they usually met during the day when she was sure Margolin wouldn't come around. How he got away from the stable in broad daylight he didn't say."

Had he, perhaps, seen Shirley Nardo during one of those trips? Been seen by her, Ellie wondered to herself?

Their food arrived, and Ellie waited impatiently while the waitress freshened up their coffee and got the detective some mustard, then plunked several additional packets of cream on the table and adjusted the menus behind the napkin container.

"Where was Mrs. Norgaard that night while her husband was in bed with Sue Anne?" she asked when the woman finally went away.

"She stayed home to take care of the horses."

"Were those always the arrangements when he went to shows?"

"No. Norgaard said she and his assistant traded off staying home."

Ellie thought she recalled L'Heureux saying something similar.

"Where was Mrs. Norgaard when you talked to Norgaard?"

"In the house, I suppose. Not around at any rate."

They discussed the reasons why Norgaard had kept the affair secret from the police, Ellie proposing that it had been silly since he should have known he'd be found out and it only made him look bad, Bieterman advancing the argument that it had been a calculated risk. "There was a good chance we wouldn't have found out, and he wouldn't have had to come clean. I'm sure he was gambling on that."

And he'd have won big if it hadn't been for her, Ellie thought but didn't say. She stacked tomatoes, dill pickles, and lettuce on top of her cheeseburger, was dumping ketchup and mustard on top of that when another question occurred to her. "Did Sue Anne give Norgaard a key to her apartment?"

"He claimed she had," Bieterman said. "Said he kept it in the drawer in his office desk, but when I asked for it, he couldn't find it, said he must have put it somewhere else. He seemed surprised when it wasn't there."

"He kept the drawer unlocked?"

Bieterman nodded.

"Trusting soul. What about Howard Margolin? Did he have a key?"

"Several," the detective said.

While Ellie considered the ramifications of this, a commotion began at the next booth as an elderly couple, loaded down with shopping bags and umbrellas, hat boxes and sweaters, tried to get comfortable. When they'd finally settled all their items on the table and benches around them, the waitress came to take their order and a shouting match ensued: one, Ellie gathered, couldn't read; the other couldn't hear. A little like Mrs. Simpson and Mr. Olson if they were to go out, Ellie thought, reminded of the elderly tenants she'd interviewed from Sue Anne's apartment complex. This reminded her of another question. "What," she asked, "is the status of those pearls missing from the apartment? Have you got a lead on them?"

"They haven't turned up yet."

"Do you have grounds to get a warrant on Margolin?"

Bieterman looked mystified. "Why? You think he has them?"

"No. But I've heard a story that certain officers at headquarters think Margolin set up the whole thing, murdered Sue Anne, then stole the pearls to throw the police off the scent."

Bieterman smiled, took a bite of his pickle. "An insurance scam, eh? I'll have to think that one over."

But Ellie could see he was more amused than intrigued. So much for Mitch and his contacts. "What about an alibi for Norgaard for the night Shirley was murdered? Does he have one?"

Bieterman nodded. "Norgaard was home with his wife. Watched television and went to bed."

Talk turned to the autopsy results on Shirley Nardo. Bieterman admitted he didn't hold out much hope the lab analysis of Shirley's car or the check of the fingerprints in her apartment would lead to much. "But you never know," he said. "We could get lucky."

"What I'd like to get lucky about is finding out what Shirley Nardo knew or saw that got her killed," Ellie said. "Got any ideas?"

"It could be anything," he said. "If the Cavanaugh woman's death was drug-related, it could be something Shirley Nardo knew about a dope deal gone sour. Or it could be that she knew something she didn't realize the significance of. There's even the possibility her death had nothing to do with the Cavanaugh woman's."

"But you don't really think that, do you?"

He wasn't going to say one way or another Ellie could tell by the look on his face. She eyed the octogenarian in the adjoining booth dozing in the sunlight streaming through the window while the wife finished his toast.

Just before they settled up the bill they discussed her phone call with Shirley Nardo. Ellie had brought along her notes, and Bieterman listened attentively as she told him what little she had written down. He'd have to see if he could locate the friend who'd dropped by, he said, tossing some bills on the table.

And, surprisingly, he gave her his cell phone number. Said he wanted to make it easier for her to reach him.

All in all, the meeting had gone well, Ellie thought as she watched him cross the street to police headquarters, turn, give her an absentminded wave before disappearing through the revolving doors. He wasn't telling her everything, but he was coming around. And what he had told her, the bit about the weekend in Salina, was something to work on.

So was the tip about the keys . . .

# CHAPTER THIRTEEN

The place was pretty full for a Thursday night, and Bieterman grabbed the last stool at the bar. He ordered a beer, glad for the feeble stream of air conditioning, glad, too, to be officially off-duty.

The Barbeque Pit doubled as a restaurant and bar—all the ribs or chicken you could eat for six-ninety-five according to the sign—but most were there for the alcohol, not the food. There were two or three tables of college students, but the majority of the people were older, and a lot of them looked like they didn't have six-ninety-five for all the ribs or chicken they could eat.

The big black woman tending bar smiled at him when he ordered another beer.

"How 'bout some ribs? Fatten you up."

He started to shake his head, then changed his mind. Soon he was working on a plate of ribs smothered in the hottest barbeque sauce he'd ever tasted.

The woman brought him a glass of water. "You a cop?"

He nodded.

She looked pleased. "I always spot 'em. You got something to do with that murder?" Again the detective nodded.

The woman cupped her chin in her hand and studied him curiously. "You gonna ask me some questions?"

This time the detective shook his head, asked her a question. "Are you Delia Jones?"

"Yes I am." She stood up and folded her arms over her ample chest.

"I've already read your statement." The detective smiled at her, and she laughed.

"Okay mister." She took his plate and moved down the counter, but she eyed him from time to time.

According to Det. Morrison, this was the place Shirley Nardo had spent her last hours, drinking beer and listening to jazz on the ancient jukebox in the corner. Witnesses said she'd been alone, had stayed until shortly before the establishment closed, hadn't talked to anybody. Those witnesses, all regulars, knew her because she was a regular of sorts herself, coming in two or three times a week either alone or with various guys. "But she was a whacko," one of them said. "Talked gibberish, ya know. Never caused trouble, but you gotta leave their kind alone." Pressed by Det. Morrison to elaborate, he explained he was referring to druggies, crazies. "We get plenty of 'em in here."

The detective caught his reflection in the mirror back of the bar. He needed a shave, could use some sleep.

Delia brought him his change. "Sad about Shirley," she said. He agreed.

Out on the sidewalk he retraced Shirley's alleged steps to where his men had found her car. The lab had found nothing of significance in the old Ford. "It'd been wiped clean," Det. Morrison had reported to him morosely. Bieterman took this as solid evidence foul play had been perpetrated in the car. What probably happened was that the murderer had followed Shirley downtown that night, parked close by, and waited in the back seat of her car while she drank in the bar. When she'd returned, drunk, and gotten in the car, he'd grabbed her from behind, strangled her from the backseat.

**116**

Then all he'd had to do was drive out to the country and dump her body in the cornfield, clean up the car and return it to its original spot. He or she, he corrected himself. He couldn't rule out a woman as the perpetrator.

So far no witness had come forward with the sighting of a vehicle parked on Barker Street between one a.m. and six, but that didn't mean he was wrong. There was little traffic down in this district, especially that late, and few people who cared to volunteer information.

Det. Bieterman angled back to his car in front of the Barbecue Pit. He could see Delia through the dirty window, hands clamped on hips, a half grin on her round face, talking to one of the customers. He started his car.

Half a mile away he parked on a side street by the Valmont. Fifty years before it had been one of the city's finest hotels, with red-coated doormen and an ornate portico in front; now it was low-income housing for the inner city poor. Rooms were forty a week, according to a sign tacked in a broken window.

A baby cried fretfully as Bieterman mounted the steps.

"Crack don't beat smack," he read on the wall while he waited in front of a door at the end of the second floor hall.

The kid's eyes, when he opened the door, were lifeless. He had dirty, straight hair, a cowlick that sprang to life over his forehead, and a runny nose.

"Bobby Hunsacker?"

The kid nodded.

"I'd like to talk to you about Shirley Nardo."

Bobby let him in.

The room had a rusty sink in the corner, a cot with a stained blanket rolled up on it, and an armchair with springs extending through the rotting base. Bieterman decided he was comfortable on his feet.

"When did you last see Miss Nardo?" he asked Bobby in

a friendly way. According to the file Bieterman had on him, the nineteen-year-old was a high school dropout who'd been picked up a couple of times for shoplifting as a minor. He'd spent a few nights in jail for possession not long ago, and other than on occasional job doing yard work or cleaning garages, he was unemployed. The reason Bieterman was there was simple. Hunsacker's fingerprints had turned out to be the ones lifted in Shirley's apartment, and the name Bobby squared with the one Shirley had used in her conversation with Ellie Schimmel.

Bobby pondered this for a while. It had been a few weeks, he said.

"That's funny. I'm told you were over at her place Sunday night."

The boy shrugged.

"What happened that night?"

They'd partied, drank, had some fun.

"She mention her friend?"

Bobby blinked. "You mean the one who got killed? Yeah. She was upset about it."

"She ever introduce you two?"

Bobby shook his head. He started to say something, then thought better of it. "Nope."

"She say much? Talk about boyfriends her friend had?"

Bobby sat down on the cot, then lay back and propped his head on his arm.

"Sick?"

"Just tired." He smiled wanly. "We got pretty wrecked that night. I'm not too sure what all she said."

Det. Bieterman sighed and extracted a bill from his wallet.

"She talked about a lotta guys this chick knew," Bobby said when the bill had changed hands. "Cowboys, I guess the chick was into cowboys. Shirl said she liked older guys, too. Sounded to me like she just liked guys, you know?" He smiled, fingering the twenty. "I think Shirl mighta been a little jealous of her, on account of she had so many guys and so much bread."

"She say that or are you making this up?"

Bobby looked insulted. "She said her friend was kind of a bitch. Didn't care who she hurt. Somethin' like that. Said she didn't used to be that way, and she thought it was a shame." He closed his eyes as if trying to remember more. "She lived with some rich guy I remember Shirl saying was a creep. Fact, she was sure the rich guy offed her."

"Either of you two get the bright idea to try to blackmail this rich guy?" Bieterman asked.

Bobby looked even more insulted. He swore under his breath.

"Shirley say something specific about why the rich guy did it?"

Bobby shook his head. "Hey man, she never said nothin' but that she hated the guy, and she wouldn't put it past him."

Bieterman changed the subject. "Where were you Tuesday night? The night Shirley got killed?"

"Prob'ly at a bar or something," he replied.

"Probably?"

"Hey man . . . "

"The Barbecue Pit?"

Bobby shook his head, wiped his nose. "No," he said. "But I'll tell you this. I wish I'd a been with Shirl, could 'a protected her or something if I'd a known."

"Known what?"

"That somebody was out to kill her." He mumbled something and then sat up.

Bieterman stared pointedly at the track marks on his skinny arms. "Kind of an expensive habit you got there, isn't it?"

Bobby stared at him impassively.

"Shirley into the heavy stuff?"

Bobby blinked a couple of times, then wiped his nose.

"How long have you and Shirley been dealing?"

Again he got no response. After with a sigh pointing out the obvious—that neither Bobby nor Shirley had any visible means of support and expensive habits to satisfy—he made the age-old threat to haul the kid downtown if he didn't get his cooperation. He repeated his original question; then, while the kid thought about it, reworded it. "You get stuff for Sue Anne, you and Shirley?"

Bobby turned indecisive eyes on him, then shrugged.

"Am I to take that as a yes?"

"Shirl might have gotten her some shit once or twice," he said sullenly. "I don't know. I never met the chick, I told you."

"So you say."

Bobby turned his head aside and refused to look at him.

"Supposing Shirley, as you said, did get her some stuff once or twice. When do you think that might have been'?"'

"I don't know."

"What's that?"

"I don't know." Bobby looked up at him uneasily, then back at the ground. "Not long ago," he said quietly. "Couple of weeks mebbee."

"She go to the Cavanaugh woman's apartment?"

"Yeah, I think so."

"You take her there?"

"I look like I can afford a car?"

Bieterman hid a smile. "Don't give me any trouble, kid. You go with her or not?"

Bobby shook his head.

"You got any idea who might have killed Shirley?"

Bobby turned his dull eyes, angry now, red-rimmed and

suddenly moist, on him. "Some son of a bitch," he said. "Some son of a bitch I'd like to get my hands on."

Touched somehow, Bieterman resisted the urge to pat him on his bony shoulder. "You aren't going anywhere soon are you?"

"Not that I know of," Bobby said dispiritedly. "Why?"

"Case I need you again," Bieterman said.

Bobby shook his head wordlessly, wiped at his nose again.

"Looks to me as if Shirley Nardo ran into somebody at the other woman's apartment one of those times she was doing her pony express routine," Bieterman said to Det. Morrison later, back at his office.

"Could be," Morrison said. "But if so, how come she didn't say anything? You just told me you didn't think she tried to blackmail Margolin, so why wouldn't she have said something to us, or even that reporter when she talked to her?"

"Like I told somebody," it must have been Ellie Schimmel, he thought, "maybe she didn't realize it was significant." Bieterman crossed to the window and opened the blinds to the darkness. "Or maybe by the time she did it was too late."

# CHAPTER FOURTEEN

Norgaard slammed the screen door behind him and headed down the darkened drive toward the barn with both dogs padding quietly behind him; within seconds, sweat gathered on his upper lip and he took off his hat, swiping at the perspiration trickling down his forehead. It was late, almost eleven, and it had cooled off some, but the humidity kept it warm.

The light above the barn entrance gradually came into sharp focus as he trudged closer; it was covered with flies, big horseflies that buzzed and swarmed around it, and he flicked it off when he got inside. He uncoiled a hose and began the drudging task of filling water buckets.

A two-year-old stud, upset at the whooshing sound the water made as it jetted into the metal bucket, laid his ears back and showed his teeth; but Norgaard paid no attention. When the horse kicked the side of his stall hard, then stood in a darkened corner and waited, ears pinned, he looked up absentmindedly. "Get back, you son-of-a-buck."

Up one aisle and down the other he went until all forty buckets were full. Then, with the practiced air of a man who'd done it hundreds, thousands of times, he recoiled the last hose, shut out the big overhead lights and went into his office.

A little later headlights shone down the lane. There were

low, chuckling sounds, a car door slammed, and someone entered the barn while the car receded into the night.

Seconds later a light flickered on in the lounge, illuminating a patch of ground outside. The television sprang to life.

It was Vogel, back from his nightly trek through the bars with Parker Davis. With a frown, Norgaard leaned back in his chair and closed his eyes. She was waiting for him over in the house, Barbara was, had been waiting for him all day and he knew why. It was because of that detective, the one in charge of Sue Anne's murder investigation. Bieterman. She wanted to know what Bieterman'd been out for, what he'd wanted with her husband so early in the morning. Why just him; why not Bart, or her for that matter? He could hear it all now, and the headache he'd nursed all day, tried to ignore, increased to an intensity that almost frightened him.

Vogel belched and changed the television channel. There were the sounds of doors opening and closing, the toilet flushed, doors again, and then quiet except for the rumbling from the television.

He supposed he should go back; he didn't want her coming after him, flicking on all the lights, attracting Vogel's attention, but inertia overwhelmed him. Dimly, by the light of the moon, he picked out the pictures on the wall opposite his desk. The one to the far left was of Norgaard himself, twenty years ago with old Snake at some show. He looked young as hell, quite serious. The one next to it was of Barbara on her barrel racer, Snuffbox, about the time he'd met her. A smaller photo, below them, was L'Heureux, around seventeen, standing up a horse for him somewhere.

His eyes brushed past Quinn with a big trophy she'd won in Columbus, Ohio, and traveled over to the far right, to the picture of Sue Anne on her mare. He ought to rip it down, smash it into a million pieces. What had possessed him? He stared for perhaps two or three minutes until a cat screeched somewhere up in the loft and startled him.

The anger dissipated and uneasiness again settled over him. His head throbbed. Wasn't there an aspirin in his drawer somewhere? Hadn't he seen one earlier when he'd been looking for his statement book? Easing open the drawer, he probed around with his hand, inched his fingers all the way to the back and felt something irregular-shaped and smooth. He pulled it out, held it up close to his face. His features changed, and for the moment, his headache no longer bothered him. It was her key. Sue Anne's apartment key.

Loud guffaws erupted from the lounge and quickly he pocketed it. Who had put it back, he wondered, after his heart stopped pounding. And when? There was no doubt that someone had; he'd torn his office apart earlier looking for it after Bieterman had asked him to produce it and he'd realized it was gone. Should he call the policeman and tell him he'd located it or, or was it better to leave things the way they currently stood?

Norgaard sat up alertly in his darkened office weighing the pros and cons. Twenty minutes later he was no closer to a decision . . .

## CHAPTER FIFTEEN

A particularly loud clap of thunder woke Ellie from a sound sleep. Sparky jumped up on her bed nervously. Winston Davis hadn't mentioned a storm in his report, she thought as lightning lit up the sky, and the noise increased. Of course weather forecasting wasn't exactly a science. She petted the dog, pulled a pillow over her head and tried to go back to sleep. At dawn she got up and made herself a cup of coffee.

It was still raining when she let herself out the front door around eight, dragging from lack of sleep.

No longer a downpour, the storm had dwindled to a steady drizzle, and she shook her head ruefully as she surveyed her geraniums. Too late for them, she thought as she dumped standing water off the tops and picked around the brown, burnt up plants for signs of life. Nothing green she could see.

At the station she joined the group, coffee cups in hands, as they discussed the storm damage and flash flooding that had swept through outlying areas during the night.

"Some cattle feeder near Hooper lost ten head," Fred Blanchard, the station's agricultural specialist, told Mitch.

"Ought to keep him humble," was the reply.

"Water washed through and drowned them faster than you can say 'Jack saw a fox.'" He was used to Mitch's sour

**125**

moods.

The Nardo funeral was scheduled for ten a.m., and before nine Mitch signaled her it was time to go. "Thank God we escape some puffball about a downed tree limb, or a power outage on grandma's farm," he said as they got in his car. "I'll take a funeral any day over that."

"What's your problem?" Ellie asked.

"That storm kept me up," he replied huffily.

Shirley Nardo's funeral was much like the Cavanaugh ceremony. Conducted in the same church, presided over by the same priest, with burial in the same cemetery, it was like having the same bad dream twice, Ellie remarked. For some reason Mitch thought that was funny. "Maybe we could use the Cavanaugh funeral tape, stick in a couple of cutaways of rain, and nobody'll be the wiser," he suggested.

Ellie shook her head and watched quietly as Mrs. Nardo and the grandfather passed, their faces obscured by an enormous umbrella. There was no Andrew.

"I'm writing this one," she told him when they got back to the station. "You'll probably pull your old copy."

The rest of the day passed slowly. A P.I. took her out mid-evening and she returned, exhausted from the humid, close air that had followed in the storm's wake. The investigation would have to proceed without her for one day, she decided when it was time to leave. She was simply too tired. She drove home slowly, let herself into the dark house, let the dog out and back in, didn't bother with anything to eat.

The next morning bright sunlight woke her from a solid night's sleep, and, with renewed energy, she decided it was time to tackle Howard Margolin. Somehow she'd get him to talk in spite of what Mitch had said. After mulling over various possibilities while she drank a cup of coffee, she called Mitch at the station. "What if I put it to him that I'm sure he's innocent, and it would be in his bet interests to tell me his story?"

"I don't know," Mitch said, sounding as irritable as he had the day before. "Do what you want. I got my own problems." The air conditioner had crapped out during the night, he explained, the one at the station. "And they got fifty clowns out here trying to get it going again. Talk about hot. And I wore my new suit."

''He's waiting for you," Margolin's secretary, Dorene, told Ellie after a short wait in the outer office of the Catamaran Lounge and led her down the hall. Ellie judged her to be around twenty, an attractive blond in a silk dress who seemed oddly reluctant to leave Ellie alone with her boss after introductions were made. She either wanted to hear their conversation, or Ellie's status as a reporter impressed her, Ellie decided.

Margolin was mixing himself a drink at his wet bar. "Dorene there told me you're doing some investigative reporting on Sue Anne's murder," he said, dropping an ice cube in his scotch. "Care for one?"

Ellie shook her head. The office was long and narrow, the man's desk at one end, a couch and several chairs grouped around a coffee table at the other. Ellie sat on the couch.

"You can go now Dorene," Margolin said. The door clicked behind her. "She also said you think I'm innocent," he continued, approaching now, looming enormous above her before he dropped into a chair. "Is that right?"

Ellie nodded. Up close, she could see that he touched up his hair to hide the grey.

"Well, I've had you checked out to be sure you aren't a lady cop, and I guess that's about as far as I can go to test your honesty, but—" Here he stopped, subjected her to close scrutiny, his expression skeptical, yet oddly amused. "I don't like to be lied to," he said, then smiled, revealing a broad space between his front teeth. "However, it really doesn't matter who you tell what to. Nobody can put me in any deeper than I already am." He shook his head and stirred his drink with his finger. "I'm about ready to sue the cops for harassment. I've got my lawyer, Gardino, looking into that, see if we have the grounds, which I think we do. Hell, business is starting to suffer because of it. I've got empty tables at eight o'clock, and that's never happened to me before. So fire away. What do you want to know?"

"Why don't we start with how you met Miss Cavanaugh."

"I ran into Sue Anne at a bar," Margolin said. "Bought her a couple of drinks, ended up taking her home. She was attracted to a combination of me and my money, like most women are."

"So that's it."

He laughed. "Sue Anne was hot stuff. She was good-looking, she was out for a good time, and she didn't want to get married. Those are my prerequisites before I hand over anything a woman can take home with her."

Cute, Ellie thought. "So you set her up at the Westshore Lake Apartments and everything was bliss until last week?"

"That's about it."

"Witnesses say you and she had a loud argument the night before she died."

Margolin continued to smile, but now Ellie thought it was a little forced. "We fought," he said matter-of-factly. "We fought a lot. No big deal, as I've been trying to convince the cops. I think Sue Anne got a charge out of it, know what I mean?"

What had they fought about, Ellie asked.

"Lots of stuff," he said. "Her spending too much money, her drinking too much, her doing drugs, her encouraging guys. She could be a real pain."

"And did she do all of those things?"

"All the time," he said.

"And on this particular night? What were you fighting about?"

Margolin's eyes narrowed. "She'd been acting funny, you know, suspicious. Like she had a secret. And she was getting a little too cocky with me, telling me how to do this and that like she owned me. I can usually tell when a woman is messing around, and she was putting out all the signs. So I accused her."

"And?"

"The usual. I was crazy, she wasn't acting anything but normal, get off her case." He shook his head. "You know, like a little kid lying to her dad. 'I didn't do it, daddy, honest I didn't,' when of course you know she did."

"Did you have any inkling who this man could have been?"

Margolin laughed low in his throat. "If I did . . ." He left the sentence unfinished. "Problem is, this guy could have been anybody. Sue Anne had guys falling all over her everywhere she went. You should have seen the reaction when she put on a bikini . . ." A slow grin spread across his face. He was attracted to Sue Anne, probably any woman, in direct proportion to the sexual interest she generated in other men, Ellie thought.

"What happened," she said, "after she denied everything that night? Did you patch things up, or leave, or what?"

"I left," he said shortly. "Told her a few things I won't repeat and came back here."

"And never spoke to her again?"

"No," he said. "I called her Saturday night, about nine or so to check in."

"Then you had decided to apologize?"

"No," he said again. "But like I told you before, she and

I fought all the time about this kind of stuff. It was nothing out of the ordinary. Fact, I told the cops to get ahold of Leanne, my ex-wife, down in Waco, she'd tell them. That's how it's always been with me and women."

What had Sue Anne had to say when he called?

"Nothing," he said. "She sounded crazy, like she'd been hitting the sauce and the pills in a big way, so I hung up. I couldn't talk to Sue Anne when she was that way. Boozed up, yeah, maybe, but when she mixed the two, forget it." He took a sip of his scotch.

"Do you know where she got her drugs?"

"The other girl that got murdered. Nardo," he said positively.

"How do you know that? Did she tell you?"

"She didn't have to. She wasn't supposed to see the Nardo chick on express orders from me, but every time she'd mention the other one, make some reference to something they did years before, she'd pull out a whole new pharmacy of crap she'd just bought somewhere. It was obvious."

"So, what happened next? You hung up because she wasn't making much sense, and you did what?"

"I stayed here at the club. You met Dorene, my secretary. She'll vouch for me. She already has to the cops."

"Your secretary works nights?"

Margolin grinned. "When necessary."

"And you were with Dorene the night Shirley Nardo was murdered?"

"That's right."

Ellie thought fleetingly again of the possibility he had murdered Sue Anne to make way for a new girlfriend. Now seemed like a good time to ask what she had witnessed between Margolin and Nardo at Sue Anne's funeral.

Margolin flushed. "She called me a couple of choice names. That's all. She hated me, I'm sure, for separating her from Sue Anne."

Ellie studied the fleshy face for signs of deception but found none. "I understand you bought Sue Anne a couple of horses," she said.

"I popped for a couple," he agreed. "Cost me a fortune. Especially when she started showing at the quarter horse deals. Hotels, food. Had to pay the owner to haul her horse." He shook his head. "And then I never saw her, off on those junkets all the time. Sometimes she'd leave on a Friday, not get back until Sunday night."

Perhaps that was when Dorene had been hired, Ellie thought. Had he ever gone along to the shows?

Once, he said, but it was so boring he came back early. "I didn't really mind the horses, that scene you understand. It gave Sue Anne something to do besides run to the bars and lay around pools soaking up a tan while I worked. The only thing I didn't like was the way some of those stud cowboys eyed her. But I took care of that. Made arrangements so she stayed with the owner's wife every show. Paid for the room myself and made it clear she stayed there or she didn't go."

Ellie got up and went over to the window so he couldn't see her face. Those arrangements had been made with Jerry Norgaard, no doubt. "Det. Bieterman mentioned some pearls you reported stolen from Sue Anne's apartment," she said. "He wanted it kept quiet for some reason, but I was wondering if you'd describe them to me. Tell me about them."

"Ten thousand I paid for them," he said. "Two years ago down in the Plaza in Kansas City. Sue Anne liked to go down there and shop. Shit. Ever hear of living to shop? That was Sue Anne. Not that I begrudged her."

Ellie turned back as he held up his hand, waved it back and forth. "The pearls had a kind of a green tint to them, and about every twelfth pearl or so they had a little diamond rondele so you could take chunks out and make them opera length or whatever. Not that Sue Anne ever went to the opera." He chuckled.

"Where did she keep them?"

"In her dresser."

"Was that all that was missing?"

"The rest of her jewelry was pretty much costume shit. She had a couple of rings, but the pearls were the only really valuable stuff."

"Were they insured?"

He frowned. "Those insurance idiots are treating me almost as bad as the cops are. When I'm cleared of this crap, they'll be down the road."

"Then you're confident you will be."

"If the cops would do their goddam job I would have been long ago," he said. "And if certain people would use their brains . . . Leanne," he said when Ellie looked puzzled. "My ex–. Remember I told you I referred the cops to her down in Texas to bolster my story? Tell them how I operate with women?"

Ellie nodded.

"Well, she called me up yesterday and confessed she told them how I choked her one time when we were in a fight. Can you believe that? All the fights we had, all the times she whacked me, what comes to mind when she sits down with the cops but the one time I got so mad I grabbed her. Can you believe it?" He shook his head. "I know what I wish I could do."

"What's that?"

"Lock that Bieterman guy up in a room with Leanne for twenty-four hours. See who's alive when I open the door. They deserve each other."

He was involved with Dorene, Ellie decided a short time later as she followed the younger woman's hip-swaying walk

**132**

back to the reception area and the exit. It could probably be proven without much effort that he'd been involved with the secretary prior to Sue Anne's murder. But did that mean anything? If Margolin took up with and discarded women as casually as rumor had it, he was merely following a long-established procedure. And no one had gotten murdered before.

"Say," Dorene said, interrupting her thoughts. "Next time you come by, bring your camera will you? I've never been on television before. Howie's always saying he's got a friend in the modeling business he's going to introduce me to, but so far nothing. Maybe if you put me on the news someone will see me, discover me, and I won't have to wait around for this friend."

# CHAPTER SIXTEEN

The Glenfield Quarter Horse Show, judging by the number of trailers and semis crowding the campground, was well-attended. Ellie had a time of it finding a spot to park her Volkswagen, finally settling for a spot in a muddy area a quarter of a mile down the road from the grandstand. She might need help getting her car out, she thought dubiously as she hiked back up the road toward the gathering.

Rich L'Heureux was brushing a grey mare in a shady area just inside the gate, his tractor cap shoved way back on his head, and she stopped.

"Rich?"

The freckle-faced hand looked up.

"Got a minute?"

He smiled. "What are you doing here?"

"I thought I'd see what a quarter horse show was all about." She perched on the sideboard of the Norgaard four-horse trailer and watched as he resumed brushing the horse's long, dark mane. Nora's Tomboy flicked her tail at the flies and chewed on the lead rope that tethered her to the side of the trailer.

"Are you showing today?"

"Jerry wants me in a halter class this morning and maybe a pleasure class this afternoon," he said, slapping the animal affectionately on her neck. He opened the trailer compartment and tossed the brush into a bucket, then pulled a hoof pick out of his back pocket and began to clean out her hooves.

"Barbara Norgaard is home, taking care of the horses, isn't that right?"

"No," he said. "She's around somewhere."

"I thought you and she took turns. You know, one of you went to the show and the other one stayed back."

"Just when it's an overnighter," he said, flicking bits of gravel and dried mud out of the horse's hoof, then letting the animal's leg drop. "Glenfield's too close." He moved around to the rear of the horse and picked up another leg. "It doesn't hurt anything when we're gone for a day. We'll be back close to feeding time. It's always worked out okay." And then, "say, I saw you on television the other night about that other woman who got murdered. Funny, Sue Anne never mentioned her before or brought her out to see her horse. They were pretty good friends, weren't they?"

Ellie nodded. They had been, she said, until Margolin had made Sue Anne stay away from the Nardo woman because he disapproved of her drug associations.

"She was into that stuff, eh?"

"That's right."

L'Heureux looked surprised. "Maybe she was killed by someone else then," he said. "Over a sour drug deal or something. Is that what the police think?"

"It's hard to say what they think. They don't say much."

Rich stood, flexing his back muscles, then stepped back and eyed the mare critically. Pleased at what he saw, he rolled down his cuffs and straightened his belt buckle, then opened the door of the pickup truck and brought out a cardboard number. "Think you could pin this on my back?"

Ellie struggled with the pin trying to force it through the

placard without sticking him in the back. "Tell me," she said as he waited patiently, crouched down so she could reach, "is Bart Vogel here?"

He chuckled.

"What's so funny?"

"Nothing. Wait'll you see him."

Ellie jabbed the pin one more time and got it through. "What do you mean by that?"

"Well, he's a little out of it," Rich said, turning now to look at her. "Some of his customers showed up to see him ride their horse, and he's been drinking ever since. Ought to be fun to see. Maybe he'll fall off."

"Is that what he usually does at shows, gets drunk and hopes for the best?"

Rich nodded. "When he gets pinned in a corner like today and has to ride. Otherwise he just goes along and comes up with some lame excuse about why the horse isn't ready."

"Did he ride in Salina, Kansas?"

L'Heureux looked thoughtful. "Let me think. I know he went along . . . " He laughed. "I don't think he even took the horse on that one. As I remember it, he spent most of his time with some of his friends in a bar. We didn't even see him."

"Who did he snare a hotel room with?"

"Jerry and me, who else? He couldn't afford to pay for one. But he was gone most of the night. I heard him stumble in just before morning and pass out on the floor." Rich grinned.

"What about the rest of you?"

L'Heureux shook his head. "Sometimes we get a little out of hand if there's a pool. Drink a few brews and make a little noise until the manager gets upset, and Jerry comes out and yells at us all to behave. But that one, no. we were all pretty tired. I think Jerry and I turned in before eleven."

And shortly after that Jerry must have snuck out for his assignation with Sue Anne, Ellie thought.

"What about Sue Anne?" she asked. "Did she go off with Bart?"

"I don't know," he said, unhooking the lead rope from the trailer, wrapping it into a neat coil. "I'm sure Margolin wasn't there. Maybe she did. The Merwalds and the Johanson woman went; Quinn Farrell went, too. Maybe she was with them. You'd have to ask around. We go and go and go, and they all blend together after a while, you know?"

The announcer's voice blared suddenly, something about three-year-old mares, and he grinned at her. "Want to come watch?"

Ellie decided she would. Keeping a respectful distance, she followed the hand and the horse through a maze of jean-clad riders and their animals. When they reached the arena gate she climbed the wooden bleachers in search of a shady spot with a good view.

Ten horses, owners at their heads, stood lined up in the center of the ring, while a judge limped slowly down the row. Jerry Norgaard was third from the end. He eyed the judge as he approached, snapped the lead rope, brought the horse's head up just at the right moment. A smattering of applause wafted from across the ring. Barbara Norgaard, leaning on the rail opposite her, was supplying that, Ellie saw. She watched as the woman made a circuitous route back to the entrance, patted her husband's arm when he left the ring with a blue ribbon in his hand. Was she aware of her husband's philandering or not? Did she even suspect?

"What the hell you doin' here?" Bart Vogel, his eyes bleary, peered down at her good-naturedly, a styrofoam cup of beer in his hand. Without waiting for an explanation he flopped down next to her with a loud grunt. He was dressed like everyone else in a long-sleeved cotton shirt, straight-legged jeans, and cowboy boots; he lacked only the cowboy hat, his dark hair slicked wetly back from his suntanned face.

"I hear you're showing this afternoon," Ellie said.

"Sure as shit am." He laughed. "See that skinny little sucker with the wife looks like a prune next to him?" He pointed out a couple in matching designer jeans and jersey tops by the refreshment stand who stared uncertainly around. "They're my own private peanut gallery here to see how I've fine-tuned their two-year-old. Shit. Sometimes we all need a little help," he held up a beer can by way of explanation, "to stay loose, not get hurt."

Ellie moved a little to the left to escape the beer vapors.

The gate opened to admit the next class and Ellie watched as Rich and the grey mare entered the arena. The spectators looked almost identical, men and women, in their jeans and long shirts with cowboy hats, and soon she'd lost sight of Rich.

"Kid doesn't know enough to get by himself," Vogel grumbled. "How the hell does he think the judge'll see him when he's got two bays and a yellow horse between him and the action?" He polished off the beer, crushed the cup, and dropped it through the planking. "Think he'd know more after all these years with Jerry."

Ellie hid a smile. "I was talking to him just a little while ago," she said. "Seems you had a wild time in Salina a few months back."

A slight smile played across his face. "God's truth, I don't remember much," he said.

"Something about you spending the night out on the town."

"That's right." He chuckled. "Pal of mine and I put that town to bed that night. Have I ever introduced you to Parker Davis, my old drinking buddy? He's around somewhere, maybe getting a horse ready to show. If I see him I'll bring him around so you can meet him."

"Would that be the man you were with the night Sue Anne's friend got murdered?" Ellie asked.

"I expect so," he said. "We go out almost every night."

"The name Shirley Nardo familiar to you?"

Bart shook his head. "I told you before, I hardly knew Sue Anne to talk to, let alone some drugged up friend of hers."

"Why do you say that?"

"What?"

"That Shirley Nardo was a drugged up friend?"

"Read it in the paper," he said casually. "The autopsy results. I can read you know."

It was curious he'd bothered to get ahold of a paper, much less keep himself informed about Shirley Nardo's murder, she thought. She got the names of his favorite bars, the ones he thought he and Parker Davis had been to the night Shirley Nardo was murdered, then steered the conversation back to the Salina show. Where had he and his friend been that night when they were putting the town to bed as he put it?

"You name it, there were women there, we were there," he said, grinning widely.

"Do you have any idea what Sue Anne was up to that night?"

Bart shook his head. "Last I remember seeing of her that night, she was in the restaurant across the street from the motel with the stable crowd, eating."

"Then you didn't invite her to go with you and Parker?"

"Nope."

" L'Heureux thought he heard you come back around daybreak and pass out."

Bart grinned. "We found us a party."

"Recall any names?"

"I'd had an awful lot even for me," he said cheerfully.

"Betty? Margot? All I remember is one of 'em was a blond and she smelled like rum and coke. And she had a big behind." He winked and leaned back in his seat. "I don't go for them skinny-hipped, flat-chested kind you see on television and in the magazine these days. Give me a woman with some meat on her bones, and I'm happy as a kid with a puppy. The rest of 'em are worthless. You know?"

Ellie turned her attention back to the ring. The ring master had everyone lined up in the center while he conferred with his assistant, a tall skinny man with a string tie. The assistant said something and the gate swung open. Soon the contestants nearest the exit departed, L'Heureux among them.

"Wouldn't you know it," Vogel snickered. "Filly could have been in the money. Would have been if Jerry'd had the good sense to show her himself. Or give her to me. That kid doesn't have what it takes."

"Was Barbara Norgaard along on that trip?"

"What trip?"

"The Salina trip."

"Nope," he said without hesitation. "She was home seeing to the stable that weekend, feeding, watering. That's what she does when Jerry goes to an overnighter. Can't leave just anybody in charge, you understand. The clients who don't show wouldn't like it. Wonder what they think when L'Heureux's in charge." He frowned. "I'm surprised Jerry and Barbara trust him, greenhorn that he is. Once or twice I stayed back when he had the place for the weekend, and I felt obliged to keep an eye on him. Left the lights on . . . didn't feed on time. I wouldn't give him all that responsibility if it were me."

Neither thought much of the other, it was obvious.

Ellie continued to watch the show.

Suddenly Bart grinned. "Say, there's Parker down there.

My buddy. Hold on a minute, I'll go get him." With the exaggerated motions of a drunk, he pulled himself to his feet, retreated down the wooden steps and hollered to his friend, a short, chubby cowboy in yellow chaps and a straw hat who was leading a horse past the stands.

Parker looked exasperated as they talked. He gestured to the horse and shook his head at Vogel, avoiding Ellie's gaze. Finally he walked away, leaving Vogel to shrug exaggeratedly in her direction.

"He's getting a horse ready," he explained when he'd made his careful way back to her side, another styrofoam cup of beer in his hand. "He's showing some horses for Randy Betts, and he said he didn't have time for conversation. Parker surprises me sometimes. You know, I didn't think of gettin' you something. Want a beer?"

Ellie wouldn't have minded a soda, but she didn't want to be responsible for Bart breaking his neck in another fraught-with-danger journey to the refreshment stand down those steep steps so she said she wasn't thirsty. That suited him fine. He nodded and lapsed into silence, concerned perhaps about his upcoming ride and how he was going to pull that off.

"We'll take a half-hour lunch break and be back with the afternoon's events, folks," the announcer squawked suddenly through the loudspeakers. Within minutes the empty arena filled with people on horseback, intent on working their animals before the ring was cleared for the afternoon's events.

Bart stirred. "Guess I oughta get down there, see what's what." But he made no move to go, eyeing the stands uneasily for his clients, sitting there like a sodden lump.

Jerry Norgaard entered the ring on the spirited black horse Ellie'd first seen when L'Heureux had been longeing it in the indoor arena. There was no mistaking the horse; it looked full of energy. Horse and rider circled first at a trot, then a few times around at a canter, then Norgaard headed

**141**

the animal through the center at a full gallop. He pulled back on the reins and the horse slid to a stop, then maneuvered the animal so that it backed up about twenty feet. Someone called to him and he waved, but he didn't stop to talk, turning the horse around and leaving the arena at a trot.

"There's Barbara," Bart said as the horse trainer's wife and a grey-haired woman in jeans and a polo shirt passed by the stands. Mrs. Norgaard looked tired and pale; she carried a sheaf of papers and a big bag, and Bart explained she was off to enter the stable's clients in the afternoon events.

"I ought to talk to her," he said. "Make sure she gets me a number," but again inertia prevailed and he sat.

"Who is that woman she's with?" Ellie asked.

Greta Johnson was her name. She kept a couple of horses at the stable, was an old friend of Barbara's, he explained. Ellie realized she hadn't seen the young girl, Quinn Farrell and asked about her. She'd been sent to summer camp for the week. "Fought tooth and nail to get out of it, but you know how parents can be," Bart said. "Her dad's a pompous son-of-a——. Doesn't like me. Guess I can't blame him. I wouldn't like a daughter of mine hanging around the likes of me, learning my bad tricks. Specially if I didn't know the guy. She's a pip for thirteen, Quinn is. Nobody can tell her how high."

Both lapsed into silence.

When the first afternoon class was called, Bart finally stood up. "Now or never," he said. "Keep your fingers crossed."

After he was gone Ellie got herself a hotdog. How did these people bear to wear such hot clothing on such a stifling day, she wondered as she passed a man in leather chaps. She knew the rationale: protective covering kept the sun from blistering the skin, but one look at the cowboy's flushed face made her wonder if it was worth it.

The rest of the afternoon passed slowly. She watched the pleasure and reining classes and left in the middle of exhibition roping when it got too close to work time.

"I tried to talk to Barbara Norgaard," she confided in Mitch when she found him alone in the newsroom, "but she didn't want anything to do with me. Gave me a glare and said she had a lot of work to do, she couldn't talk. About the only thing I got out of her was that she didn't know Shirley Nardo. None of them did. By them, I guess she meant the stable crowd."

Mitch yawned. This, of course, was the first he'd heard of the affair between Sue Anne and the horse trainer, and his reaction wasn't what she'd expected. So what, he seemed to say. People had affairs all the time.

"I think Bart might know," she mused. "He claims he was gone all night at the Salina show, but maybe he and his friend knocked on Sue Anne's door during their partying, or saw Norgaard sneaking back to the motel room. It would explain why Norgaard lets him stick around. And L'Heureux. He claims they both went to bed early. It's possible if he heard Bart coming in early in the morning, he heard Norgaard, too . . ."

"You're wasting your time," Mitch pronounced. And then he voiced what she suspected. "So what if they had a little thing going. I still say it's Margolin." And he asked whether she'd been successful in getting an interview with him.

Ellie recounted her talk with Margolin, explained how she'd gotten in, and Mitch shook his head in disbelief.

Ellie went back to her desk and sat down. The memory of Bart Vogel in the Junior Pleasure class came to mind, and she smiled. The horse was running away from him, someone had snickered behind her as she'd watched from the rail.

"Look at number 329. Is that Vogel? That filly's going to

**143**

throw him clear over the fence." Vogel had looked like a sack of potatoes flung up on the horse's back. Ellie could hear the man grunt each time they raced by, Vogel hunkered forward over the horse's neck, the animal wild-eyed with the bit between her teeth. But he'd hung on, not been thrown, had made it to the lineup before he'd been dismissed.

"Needs a little more work," she'd heard him telling the owners at the gate after the class. "Let me keep her another month, see what I can do with her." He was swaggering by then, no doubt relieved he'd stayed on, made it through the ordeal. Now he was bargaining for a little lead time, the chance to do some business. Ellie hadn't waited around for their decision.

He'd talked them into it, she thought now as the phone on her desk began to ring. There had been something too gullible in their expressions, something too knowing in his for her to think otherwise. How long, she wondered, would he be able to stay on that tightrope? And how could people be so easily duped? She didn't know, really, what to make of Bart Vogel.

# CHAPTER SEVENTEEN

Det. Bieterman turned on the window air unit in his back bedroom and opened the door to the kitchen in hopes it could handle both rooms. Fans usually sufficed—he liked warm, fresh air— but the humidity sometimes made it impossible to breathe. He listened to the rattling sound from the ancient machine and prayed it would last through the day. It was his day off and provided he could keep the house from turning into an oven, he planned to stay home.

A newspaper feature on Canadian fishing caught his eye, and he sat hunched over the kitchen table in his gym shorts, wishing he was there. He'd used up all his vacation time in Aspen skiing. He frowned, rubbed at a knee that was still bothering him five months after he'd taken a particularly bad fall on an icy stretch. Cpt. Borden had told him forty was too old for rough sports like skiing, that he'd better take up something like golf, and he'd thought, why, so I can get fat? He liked to keep in shape, and he'd been skiing since he was a child. Not to mention he was always ready for action, found it difficult to relax without lots of physical activity. Anybody could fall; it had nothing to do with age, he'd told the captain.

Maybe he'd go out and mow the yard, he thought as he peered out the back window at the knee-deep grass between the house and the old garage. Then again, maybe he'd just watch some baseball, try to rest. He'd fry up some chicken later, make a big bowl of potato salad.

The phone rang. It was Det. Morrison. He hated to bother him on his day off, but some information had come to light he thought the detective ought to know about. Bieterman sighed. On his way out, he turned off the air conditioner.

Thirty minutes later when he walked into the office, Det. Morrison was sitting there looking enthused, his big, broad face hopeful. "They've found a couple of saddles," he said. "And this George Quinlan identified them."

Bieterman closed the door, leaned against it. "Who's he?"

"The guy's former employer," he explained patiently. "Some rich man just outside of Norman, Oklahoma who owned a thirty-stall horse barn and almost half a million dollars worth of quarter horses. Can you imagine having money like that for a hobby?" he asked wonderingly. "Anyway, this Quinlan had reported the missing saddles to his insurance company but hadn't bothered with the authorities because by the time he'd discovered them gone he'd figured the trail was cold. Typical. Just didn't want to be bothered," he said. "There they were in a western store in Norman, right in the front window. And the guy who bought them acted surprised as hell they were hot."

"Can he make a positive I.D. of who sold them to him?"

Morrison laughed. "The guy's a friend of his."

Det. Bieterman sat down at his desk. "Anything else missing?"

"Yeah. A couple of bridles and another saddle. We're in luck."

"You start any of the paperwork?"

Morrison nodded. "Bet there's plenty more where that came from."

Bieterman sighed. They'd need a warrant which would take some time. Morrison was still standing there and Bieterman frowned. "What are you waiting for?"

"Say listen. This pans out, what say you buy me a steak dinner at Lyman's. With a baked potato, sour cream, one of their nice Italian salads, the works."

"What for?"

"For working so hard. Missing out on too many home-cooked meals lately."

Bieterman frowned. "You think I owe you something, eh?"

Morrison grinned. "You said it."

"What makes you so sure we've hit pay dirt? The guy's a crook, so what?"

Morrison pressed his hands together as if in prayer. "I'm making deals," he said.

Bieterman shook his head. "Oh, well. In that case." Sure, he'd take him out to dinner. He'd take Lila, too.

"And the kids?"

"No. Not the kids." He didn't think the wager of two free meals was sticking his neck out so far, but seven . . . "You and Lila, that's it."

"You're on." Morrison slammed the door behind him.

# CHAPTER EIGHTEEN

"What'd you find out?"

"A few things," Ellie said, wishing now she'd ordered a sandwich like her sister instead of the unappetizing salad the waitress set in front of her. "It was worth the phone call." They were eating at a new restaurant on Kansas Avenue; Todo's it was called, after Dorothy's dog. They had stood in line for the better part of an hour in front of the place and now, finally, were tasting the fruits of their overly long wait.

"I told you they were known for the Reuben sandwiches," Phoebe said. "Here take half of mine."

Ellie shook her head and forked another bite of the "Todo Tuna Trip" into her mouth. The funnel clouds on the walls were too much, she thought; so were the old-fashioned dirndls and ruby-red shoes the waitresses wore. "Barbara Norgaard's maiden name was Stratlin," she said. "She's from Billings, Montana, the only daughter of a rancher who died a few years ago, and her mother lives in a nursing home in Billings. Has rheumatoid arthritis or something."

"Will she inherit?"

"I imagine so if the mother doesn't live too long. But I don't gather there's much to inherit according to Mrs. Johnson."

"That friend of Barbara Norgaard's you called?"

"Right." Greta Johnson had been a wealth of information, the kind of woman who loved to talk on the telephone. "I've boarded horses with the Norgaards for years now," she'd said briskly. "Barbara's one of my closest friends."

"What about Jerry Norgaard?" Phoebe interrupted. "What'd she say about him?"

"Honest but poor from what she's heard. The Stratlins gave the couple some money when they first married; but his reputation made it mushroom. Mrs. Johnson went on and on about what a pillar of the horse community he is. She said there are plenty of seedy horse trainers out there, but he's not one of them. People bring their horses from five states away for him to train." Ellie broke a roll and buttered it. She took a bite. "I've been trying to picture what would happen to the Norgaards financially if they were to have divorced. If Jerry Norgaard were to have left his wife for Sue Anne. If he's as reputable as everyone says, and as remorseful as Bieterman thinks, he'd probably have left the house and land to Barbara, gone off on his own and tried to start over. He'd have had to find a bank to lend him money, buy or lease land, put up a barn . . . it would have taken years to reestablish himself, and I don't see Sue Anne living in a trailer, do you?"

Phoebe looked up matter-of-factly. "In a pig's eye."

"It wouldn't have been quite as hard on Barbara Norgaard," she continued thoughtfully. "Provided she was willing to go back to work full-time running the place. Provided, too, that L'Heureux would have stayed with her and kept up his end. But I don't imagine it would have been something she'd have relished. And I don't think Rich has experience training." Ellie squeezed lemon in her iced tea. "Mrs. Johnson told me something else I found interesting. She didn't know about Norgaard and Sue Anne or I'd have heard about it, believe me. But, listen to this: someone told her once that Barbara Norgaard and Bart Vogel used to be an item. She

**149**

couldn't remember where she'd heard it, didn't know any of the particulars, but she swore someone told her once that they'd dated years ago before she married Jerry Norgaard." Ellie took another bite of her salad, helped herself to another roll. "I wish the Johnson woman had known more about it. I'd like to talk to that young girl, Quinn Farrell. But I can't. She's at camp for the rest of the week."

"Why do you think she'd be helpful?"

"Well, I don't know that she'd have heard anything about Barbara Norgaard and Bart Vogel, but she's out there from sunup to sundown, just the sort to have overheard something. And from the way Bart referred to her, I got the impression they were pals. At the very least, she might be able to tell me more about him."

Phoebe beckoned to the waitress and asked for more iced tea. "I read in the paper where Shirley Nardo only weighed eighty-five pounds."

Ellie nodded. "At that weight just about anybody could have carried her into that cornfield and dumped her. It wouldn't have to have been a man."

"Never thought of that. You're right. Suppose the wife did it? It's possible." She stared at Ellie. "Eighty-five pounds. God. I haven't weighed anything close to that since I was in the fourth grade. You weren't exaggerating when you said she was a wreck. How can people do that to themselves? Become addicts. Let drugs take over their lives like that. It's pathetic."

"I don't know. But she was definitely in over her head."

They ate in silence for a while. It wasn't until they had both ordered chocolate cake for dessert, and Ellie had cheered up after sampling it—at least the entire meal wasn't a disaster—that Phoebe mentioned she'd talked to their parents.

"Last night," she said, scraping some frosting off her portion. "You're supposed to call them."

"Why?"

"They're worried about what you're up to. You know, the fact that we went to school with Sue Anne and Shirley, and you're so involved in the whole thing. I think they're afraid you might be in danger."

"You told them that was absurd."

"Sure. But you know how much that helps. I pointed out you were a big girl, you were working closely with the police, they would watch out for you, the works. They still want you to call."

Ellie made a face.

"Speaking of calls, have you ever phoned Gordon, found out what his problem is?"

Ellie shook her head. "Why should I?"

"I don't know. Maybe he's tried to get in touch with you and been unable to find you. You aren't that easy to contact, you know. You're never home. You don't answer your phone. You're so tied up with these murders and all. And when I've called you at the station, nobody ever seems to give you the message."

Ellie grimaced. Gordon had made no attempt to call her. She knew that for sure. "Mom would die if she knew what was going on wouldn't she?" she said lightly. "After two years of harping at me for living with him, the shoe'd be on the other foot if she thought I was being dumped, wouldn't it?" And she changed the subject, segueing smoothly into a question about her two nephews. At least she'd warded off further conversation about Gordon, she thought soberly, as she listened to her sister describe how exhausting two small boys could be, especially when their father worked late every night, arrived home after they were safely in bed. "I can't wait for fall and school. I wasn't made to be a full-time mother."

Fall. Crisp weather, autumn colors, apple cider. It was something to look forward to. Ellie thought about that and tried to dismiss the feelings Phoebe's mention of Gordon had brought on. Football games, sweaters, leaf raking . . . By then she'd know one way or another where she stood with Gordon. Surely he'd contact her by then.

"Next time I'll pick the restaurant," she said firmly as they made ready to leave. "We'll go to a cafe or a diner or something and have a burger."

"If you'd have ordered a Reuben like I told you to, you'd have liked the place," Phoebe retorted. "But you never have been one to listen."

# CHAPTER NINETEEN

Through the plastic bag it looked like the sort of thing a young girl would play dress-up with, stand in front of a full-length mirror and twirl this way and that. It was only when it was taken out and held up to the light, the diamond chips twinkling colorfully, the small greenish-beige stones heavy in the hand, that one sensed its worth.

Det. Morrison was whistling something under his breath, and Bieterman stifled the urge to tell him to can it.

"Wish things went this way more often," he said suddenly. "Makes a man look forward to coming to work. Builds up an appetite, too."

Det. Bieterman stuffed his hands in his pockets and leaned back in his chair, trying hard to ignore him. Who'd have thought the guy would have left the strand in the glove compartment of his pickup?

"Found a couple of silver-inlaid bridles in a trunk in the back, too," Det. Morrison chortled. "I'll bet you another steak dinner they're George Quinlan's."

"How'd he seem when you picked him up?"

"What?"

"How'd he react when you brought him in? Found the stuff?"

"I don't know. Surprised I guess."

"Surprised like he'd never seen the stuff before or sur-

**153**

prised like he couldn't believe he got caught?"

"If I had to say, I'd pick the second one, I guess. Hell, I don't know. What difference does it make? We got him down the hall waiting for you. Ask him yourself."

"I'm in interrogation for at least an hour," Bieterman told the detective in the next office as he and Morrison headed that way. "Take my calls will you?"

Two turns later he paused, tucked in his shirt then opened the door. The old-fashioned ceiling tiles punctured with holes always reminded him of school, of leaning back in his seat and counting them for something to do. So did the dirty green walls.

"Good afternoon," he said briskly to the man sitting at the scarred table in front of him. "I understand you've been Miranda'd and don't feel you need the services of an attorney at this time. Is that correct?"

The man nodded. He was clearly scared; he shifted awkwardly in the metal chair and waited for the officer's lead like a naughty boy caught with a spit wad.

"Well then. How about we start by you explaining to me how you got these?" Bieterman held up the plastic container with the pearl necklace inside it.

The man grinned uncertainly. "It ain't what you think."

"What I think doesn't matter. What I know is this pearl necklace belonged to Sue Anne Cavanaugh. She, as we all know, happens to be dead. Murdered. So. How about we start by you explaining to me how you got this," he said again.

Bart Vogel cleared his throat.

"I had nothing to do with killing her," he said. He sat up straighter, passed a shaking hand across his face. "You gotta believe that. I only wanted the pearls. I've hit on hard times . . ."

Bieterman and Morrison exchanged looks. No need for

their usual routine, Bieterman said with his eyes. Just keep quiet and let the man talk.

"I don't know who killed her," he said again to silence. "I only copped the pearls." After a few minutes of silence, he opened up. He'd first seen them one night when he'd run into her at a bar on Benson Drive, he said, mentioning a well-known nightclub midtown. "She was all decked out in some slinky low cut dress with them around her neck" he said, pointing to the plastic bag on the table between them. It didn't take a genius to know they were real and worth something. Immediately the idea of stealing them and passing them on to a friend to fence had occurred to him.

"The friend's name?"

"Guess there's no reason not to tell you since he never did anything. Parker Davis."

"He make it a habit to receive stolen goods?" This, dryly, from Morrison drew a warning frown from Bieterman.

He skirted the question. He and Parker had made their plans one night late after a day of drinking, he said. It wouldn't be all that difficult they'd reasoned. Just wait until she left, go in, grab the thing, and leave.

"What about the doorman and the apartment door between you and the pearls?"

Bart's reply was low; he avoided their stares. "I had a key. Actually, I knew where I could get a key." His source, of course, was Jerry Norgaard. Norgaard had been messing around with the girl, he said rapidly; he'd seen all he needed to at the Salina show to be convinced of that. All he'd had to do was go through Norgaard's desk one night to find the key. "The doorman was no problem either," he added. "I just waited until he took a break, slipped in and went up the back stairs."

"Anyone see you? You see anyone?"

He shook his head.

"Go on."

He'd worn gloves on Parker's advice. Experienced no trouble finding the pearls in the top drawer of her dresser. He didn't take anything else because he didn't want to press his luck, and he figured she might think she mislaid them, at least for a while. Always loaded she was, and flaky as hell . . . He took a deep breath, kneaded his knuckles.

He was just about to open the door when he heard her in the hall, fumbling with the lock. Off he'd hightailed it to the sliding glass doors and let himself out onto the balcony, stood pressed tightly against the wall out of her view until she'd passed through the living room and gone down the hall.

"At that point I got outta there. Shit. I was sweatin' so bad I'm surprised she didn't smell me. What the hell was she doing there, I kept wondering. She was supposed to be at the club with Margolin. That's where she always was."

Det. Bieterman kept a straight face; he didn't look to see how Morrison was responding.

"The stupid thing I did was leave the sliding glass door open. I was so scared and in such a hurry I didn't take the time to close it. Not that I guess it mattered much anyway, on account of what happened later. Her getting murdered I mean. Even if she found the door open, it didn't do her any good."

"Let me be sure I'm following this," Bieterman said. "Miss Cavanaugh was alive and well when you left with the pearls. You saw her pass through the living room, presumably heading down the hall to the bedroom just before you left, leaving the balcony doors open."

"That's right. Close to eight it was by then." Vogel's expression was open but anxious.

"And you never went back there."

"No sir."

"Where did you go?"

"I got the hell out of there. Rode the elevator down to the parking garage, snuck up the ramp, drove off in my truck."

"And the pearls? Why didn't you dispose of them as planned? Or dump them somewhere?"

"Parker wouldn't touch them with a ten foot pole after he heard about the murder. And they were just too beautiful to get rid of like Parker told me to. I figured, lay low, wait it out, get my money's worth later after the hoopla died down. Guess I didn't think too clearly. I did put the key back, just the other night."

Morrison and Bieterman exchanged looks. Morrison spoke first. "Sounds pretty coincidental to me, the same night two penny-ante crooks like you and this Parker Davis steal a string of pearls from this girl, somebody else comes in on your heels and strangles her?"

Bart didn't take offense. "I'm telling the truth, sir. I know it sounds crazy, but that's how it happened. I somehow figured it would come to this. You'd get me and say I did it because of the pearls. But I didn't. I swear I didn't. I was only after the pearls, and the girl was fine when I left."

"Where can we find Parker Davis? See if he confirms any of this."

Vogel looked uncomfortable. "You gotta talk to him, eh? He didn't do anything, really. Never fenced the pearls, told me I should come clean even. Do me a favor then," he said when he realized it was going to be. "Don't tell him I said anything about him, would ya? Just let him think you put two and two together. You know, people saw us together so you picked him up for questioning, something like that. I'd sure appreciate it. He's my buddy, you know."

Where did he get the impression he had bargaining power, Bieterman wondered as he gave Morrison the signal to leave, find the friend. "Take it easy, Mr. Vogel," he said in the next breath. "Let's see if we can't hammer out your statement and get it signed before your friend gets here."

There was no way he could have known about the door being left open had he not been there, he thought as Bart nodded unwillingly. Then, too, he couldn't have known when she'd returned to the apartment. The girl must have stayed in the bedroom most of the evening getting stoned, weaving only as far as the galley kitchen for ice cubes and whiskey, leaving the living room dark. Failing to notice the open doors, the 85° humid air wafting in. "Let's run through this again, shall we?" he said. "Start with how you got to the Westshore Lake Apartments. You drove, eh? Parked right out in front?"

# CHAPTER TWENTY

The skimmers were full of leaves and bugs, the sucking sounds they made unpleasant, like someone gasping for breath, and Barbara Norgaard emptied them behind a bordering shrub. The pampas grass around the diving board was taking over, crowding out the freesia and delphiniums, she noticed, but she didn't care, couldn't work up the energy to care. Maybe in the fall, she thought, sinking wearily into a lawn chair, studying her freckled legs and curled toes. Not a cloud smudged the blue sky, and she pulled sunglasses out of her bag, lay back and closed her eyes. She could hear a cardinal in the bushes making his loud call, then a chickadee with his chick-a-dee-dee-dee-dee.

A few seconds later a horse whinnied from an outdoor pen, then squealed, the hoof beats on the packed earth dull and faraway. She sighed and resettled herself, feeling the sun as it began to bake her skin. Eventually she dozed. The nap ended abruptly when a car door slammed on the other side of the privacy fence. Sitting up in some confusion, she waited and, seconds later, Ellie Schimmel appeared at the gate. Carefully she arranged her features into a pleasant expression.

She was uptight, Ellie thought as she took the chair the woman indicated. A large straw hat covered the woman's hair, and the one-piece bathing suit she wore outlined in even sharper detail her thin, boyish frame. If anything she was thinner than before, Ellie thought, her collarbones jutting out at uncomfortable angles, dark smudges under her eyes exposed when she pulled off her sunglasses to squint at Ellie.

"You've heard about Bart, haven't you? That he's been arrested in the Cavanaugh case?"

Barbara Norgaard nodded. "I was here when they came out and got him."

"You must have been quite surprised." When that didn't illicit a response, Ellie got to the point about why she was there. "I heard that you and he dated at one time."

Two red spots appeared high on her cheekbones, and she looked discomfited. After a long silence, she spoke. Choosing her words carefully, she said: "We did date once, but I don't see why it would matter." She gazed at the crystal-clear water in the pool, then back at Ellie. When Ellie remained silent, she spoke. "I was eighteen, he was nineteen or twenty. We met at a horse show and dated a few months. He was good looking back then, and as I said, I was young . . . Eventually we drifted apart. I met Jerry. He met another girl. That's about it."

"Was he training horses?"

She nodded. "He was training and showing a lot. He always had clients, always seemed to make do. In fact, he really didn't get to be the way he is now until about five years ago. A horse went over on him and broke his hip. Jerry told me he spent half a year in a hospital recuperating; and when he got on again, a horse I mean, he'd lost it, he was afraid. That, apparently, brought on the drinking." She didn't look sorry about this. "He's a fool," she said. "I told you that before. Weak. Cares about nobody but himself. I gather he murdered the girl when she caught him in her apartment. I doubt he meant to do it, he probably panicked."

**160**

"Then you believe he murdered Miss Cavanaugh?"

The older woman looked at her. "Well, of course. Don't you?"

Ellie shrugged, smacked a mosquito that lit on her arm. "Tell me why your husband has put him up for so long," she said. "I've heard rumors he's been stealing equipment, he never pays for anything, and yet Mr. Norgaard continues to let him board his horse here, bring in clients. Why's that?"

Barbara Norgaard's head lifted at this, anger flashing briefly across her face, but then her head bowed and the hat shrouded her face. "Jerry has always been more . . . tolerant," she said uncertainly. "I think because he's felt sorry for him, down on his luck and all."

"But you haven't?"

"I don't look at it as bad luck. He gave up. And he was always too busy running after women, taking advantage of people." Her voice trailed off.

"Is that what he did with you?" Ellie asked softly. "Took advantage of you, then ran off with someone else?"

Mrs. Norgaard got up, went over the pool and splashed a few drops of water on her arms. She took off the straw hat and dabbed at her temples. When she came back, there was a curious half-smile on her face. "In a way, yes. We dated for a few months, and then one day he left me high and dry. Took off on a three month circuit with another girl, didn't even tell me he was going. I've never been able to forgive him, even now, as ridiculous as he is," she said. "It was embarrassing with everyone knowing, and then, I was sure I was in love with him. I was broken-hearted. I thought my life was over. Of course it wasn't. I met Jerry, we got married. It all worked out for the best. Still, I've never been able to forgive Bart. There's just something in me that boils up every time I see him. You'd think, after all this time . . ."

She took off her hat, fluffed up her hair, her freckles

**161**

standing out sharply on her white face. "We've seen Bart at shows over the years, and he's stayed a night or two before when he was passing through. But this time . . . well, I guess Jerry felt bad about what's happened. The way I look at it, if he hadn't let him stay here, he wouldn't have met Miss Cavanaugh and then . . ." She left the sentence unfinished, eyed Ellie as though gauging her reaction. "Not that anyone could say Jerry's responsible. He's provided him with a place to stay, eased his financial problems for him. Bart . . . he's the one who got himself into trouble."

"Your husband is an awful nice guy," Ellie said.

Mrs. Norgaard pulled a cigarette out of her handbag and lit it. She took her time about it, holding the lighter to the end with a shaking hand, staring hard at Ellie all the while. Finally she spoke. "I guess I'm going to have to level with you about something, because if you don't already know, you're going to find it out. My husband's not that nice of a guy. The truth is Bart found out Jerry was having an affair with the Cavanaugh woman. Teased Jerry about it, he'd tell me, something like that." She stared off at the shimmering water, her eyes smoldering. "Your next question's going to be, how do I know this. Did Jerry tell me? The answer to that is no." She took a drag on her cigarette, blew out the smoke in one rapid puff.

"Jerry acted guilty, became self-absorbed, there was just something I picked up on. So I did a little investigating on my own. Listened in on a few telephone conversations, followed him over to her place a couple of times. It started at the Salina show, I think. Bart found out then, probably. Jerry was sharing a room with him that weekend, and he missed him during the night or something." She shook her head angrily, drew in another lungful of smoke, expelled it. "Pretty ironic my ex-lover would be one of the first to know my husband was unfaithful to me, don't you think. And that I've had to act like I didn't know, didn't care." She drew on her sunglasses and leaned back in her chair. "I don't know why I'm telling you all this. Jerry doesn't even know I've figured it out."

The silence grew long.

"I don't think it was out and out blackmail," she said finally. "Bart's not like that. It was more the elbow-digging, coughing, knowing-looks type of routine, if I know Bart. Probably had Jerry totally cowed."

She sat, motionless, said no more.

Ellie cleared her throat. "Where is your husband right now?" she asked.

"He's in the house, resting. He hates being out in the sun in the afternoon. And this whole thing, the murder, the investigation, Bart's arrest, have been really hard on him. He's not taking it well."

"Does he think Bart murdered Sue Anne, too?"

The older woman turned her head to look at Ellie. "Well, of course. I mean, I suppose so. We haven't really discussed it . . . The girl came in, as I said, and he panicked. Or, he went in expecting to find the place empty, and there she was. The calculating little . . ." She took a deep breath, and then, "What will the police do with Bart now?"

"I'm not the one to ask," Ellie replied. "He hasn't been charged with anything yet." Before she'd driven out here she'd headed to Bieterman's office, asked the same question and he'd shrugged, told her he couldn't say. Only that Vogel had admitted to burglary, and that was off the record. A thought occurred to Ellie now and she voiced it. "What about the Nardo woman? Do you believe Vogel killed her, too?"

Barbara Norgaard took off her sunglasses and stared at Ellie. She looked puzzled, like she hadn't thought about that and wasn't sure. But then she got a resolute look on her face and she said, "I think we've talked enough, you and I. It's about time for you to go."

"Could I talk to your husband?"

''He's resting," she said again, firmly.

Why was the woman being so protective, Ellie wondered as Mrs. Norgaard stubbed out her cigarette and then, abruptly, stood up, said she was going to take a swim. Was the horse trainer really napping in there as she said, or avoiding Ellie? And under whose orders?

Mrs. Norgaard doffed her hat, strode to the deep end, and dove into the pool, cutting through the water with clean, energetic strokes. She exercised regularly, Ellie thought, as the woman's small, muscular body churned up the water into a frothy tangle. She was lithe and agile, and it struck Ellie that she might even be stronger than her husband.

Ellie gathered up her things to go. Mrs. Norgaard continued to lap the pool, stroking hard, with no sign of a letup. Had she really kept the knowledge of her husband's affair to herself? It was possible, but why? Why not have it out with him, get it over with, find out where she stood? Too many questions, too few answers. Ellie sighed, headed for her car.

As she drove down the gravel road, reliving their conversation, a ramshackle farmhouse on the opposite side of the road caught her attention and she experienced a flashback. Suddenly it was winter, dark, crusty patches of snow faintly visible. She was dressed warmly in a black parka and a hat, heavy boots and socks, and she picked her way carefully, afraid she might slip on a patch of ice. Having thought all the lights in the farmhouse were out, she was surprised to see a light on in the back as she got closer, maybe in the kitchen, and she wavered for a minute. Was someone still up or had the light merely been left on?

And then she saw a slight movement near the front porch steps and she made the decision to keep going. She walked more quickly now, praying no one heard her faint, crunching footsteps. The cold wind was in her favor she thought. With the windchill, it was twenty below, and she shivered involuntarily. Clouds covered the moon and made visibility poor. She kept her head down and her gloved hands in her pockets. Watching the farmhouse for any signs of movement inside, she dropped down on her knees and crawled the last few feet to the steps leading up to the front porch.

A slight whimper greeted her over the wind. Now she could faintly see the animal, crouched in a ball against the cold, shivering imperceptibly. A black and white dog, its back legs frozen in a pool of ice, a chain wound tightly around its neck. The taut chain extended to a hook in the ground to which it was firmly tethered. The animal was emaciated, its hollow eyes watching her as she leaned over it, fumbling in her large coat for wire cutters. She cut the chain and as she did, the animal lifted its head and licked her gloved hand. She patted its muzzle reassuringly and coaxed it to stand. It couldn't. It was frozen in place.

Ellie impulsively swung the wire cutter at the frozen puddle several times with quick motions and chipped the animal free. With that, she scooped the dog up and sprinted off, no time to worry about the noise she had made, intent only on getting away from the house and yard and back to the road. A few seconds later a porch light flicked on.

Keeping her head down, and trotting now, she kept going, frightened but determined. The starved dog was light, and, fortunately, she had made it to the road and her car before the clouds parted and the moon lit up the area. Without looking back, she jumped in the car and took off, dog in her lap, headlights off. Not until she was a few miles away did she dare to move the animal to the passenger seat and flick the car lights on. The animal made no sound, but his eyes followed her. And then, as if he knew he'd been saved, he rested his head in her lap and closed his eyes. She stomped down on the accelerator and got the hell out of there.

Her first rescue. Prompted by a friend's description of the dog's plight after he'd stopped at the farmhouse to get directions to a boarding kennel nearby. She'd found out exactly where this farmhouse was and decided to take the suffering animal when she couldn't get the image of the poor thing out of her mind. She'd told no one. It had been Sparky, of course.

She'd never been traced, meaning whoever had turned on that porch light hadn't gotten the numbers off her plates. Sparky had recovered after a few months of food and tender care. And that had triggered her call to a rescue organization. She wanted to help, she'd told the woman on the other end of the line. She couldn't foster animals or ferry them from puppy mill rescues, or do any of the myriad other things they undoubtedly did to rescue dogs, but she'd be willing to snatch abused dogs, no questions asked. After a stupefied silence, the woman had said of course. And her clandestine missions had begun. Whenever a report of an abused dog came in, the director of the rescue organization called her with the address and the particulars and she did the rest. Always at night when the darkness protected her.

## CHAPTER TWENTY-ONE

"We back to square one again, Sam?" Morrison leaned against the wall of Bieterman's office, arms crossed, legs splayed, a dour look on his face. "That cowboy telling the truth?"

Det. Bieterman rifled around in the back of his drawer, found a packet of sugar that had been there for years from the crunchiness of it, dumped it into a cup of steaming coffee. "Which cowboy are you talking about? Vogel or his pal?"

"Take your pick."

Parker Davis hadn't been difficult to find. Sitting at the Midwest Bar on the Benson Parkway with a can of Pabst Blue Ribbon in front of him, he'd come along shamefacedly with Morrison, had talked freely. Vociferous in his denial that he'd planned to fence the stolen pearls—Vogel was a liar—he had, however, conceded that during the course of one drunken get together Bart had expressed the desire to lift the jewelry, had specified the date and the time despite his earnest protestations. "I 'tole the idiot he was gonna get caught, but a fool's born every minute, they always say." Hearing that the girl had later been murdered, he claimed he told Vogel to come clean. "Better to be caught with stolen goods, than have a murder rap pinned on ya." But his friend hadn't listened.

**167**

"Their stories match," Bieterman said now. "I wouldn't go so far as to say we're back to nothing. We've cleared up the burglary, and we know the strand disappeared the same night the murder took place. We also have Parker Davis describing the night they hatched their plot as a drunken one, with much loud discussion." *We was at the Midwest Bar, I think,* Parker had said. *Nah, it was later, back in the lounge where Vogel's been stayin. He was so out of it . . . drinkin' since mebbe two that afternoon, talkin' loud like we was discussin' some two-year-old filly or something. I had to tell him to shut up more'n once.* It had been late—ten or eleven o'clock, he thought.

"Somebody clearly overheard them if he's telling the truth."

Morrison shifted his feet, stared out the window. Gradually his expression became more cheerful. "Could be," he said. "We know what weekend it was?"

"Shouldn't be too difficult to find out."

"Think that'll help?"

"Ought to be able to narrow down the list of suspects considerably."

Morrison started to whistle. Bieterman took a large swallow of coffee.

"How come I didn't think of that?" Morrison asked after he finished his tune.

Bieterman smiled. "You were too busy feeling sorry for yourself over that steak dinner you lost out on."

Morrison shot him a withering glance and shook his head. It still counted, he said. He was still entitled to that meal. So was Lila. Hadn't Bieterman just said bringing in Vogel had helped narrow the field considerably?

The phone rang, cutting off further discussion.

## CHAPTER TWENTY-TWO

"I will mother. Right. I'll tell her. Give Dad a kiss." Ellie clicked off her phone, glad that was over. She folded the afghan crumpled on the couch and carted the dishes from last night's dinner into the kitchen, dumping them into the sink and adding soap and hot water. Parents. Why did they have to be so difficult? Treat their grown children as if they were still under their wings?

"You'd be better off leaving police work to the police," her mother had said. "I don't think you grasp the danger you're putting yourself into."

"You want me to seal myself off in a cocoon?" Ellie'd been tempted to crack but hadn't. She'd be all right, she'd said instead. She wouldn't do anything foolish.

And then her mother had asked about Gordon. Not in an interested way as if she cared, more in an off-hand manner akin to wondering whether her car was still running. He was busy, she'd said; he was still getting used to New York and so on. And the conversation had turned again, this time to Phoebe and the two boys.

How on earth was Gordon, she wondered now? She dried the plates, stacked the clean glasses. Had he married the grad assistant by now? She went into the dining room, thumbed through the latest *Sentinel* stacked on top of a week's worth of back issues she'd never gotten to. Why didn't he have the decency, no, the courage to tell her he'd found someone else when it was so painfully obvious. Sonya, Tonya, what was her name? Didn't a person usually do that at least? Apologize, sound a bit rueful?

Hancock had a front page story again, she noticed as the bold headline penetrated. **COWBOY ARRESTED.** She skimmed the article. He wrote well, she saw, didn't force his readers to wade through paragraph after paragraph to get the whole story like some of those newspaper reporters. A photograph of Det. Bieterman accompanied the article. Sitting stiffly at his desk, he looked too posed, one of those studied looks she thought all officials practiced so people would take them seriously, feel the confidence they exuded and be reassured. He could have smiled, she thought, made himself look a little more human. It didn't have to be a leer, just a faint grin.

She tossed the old newspapers out, got ready to leave. Sparky looked like he knew, followed her.

He was scared to call her, she admitted wearily, thinking of Gordon again. Either that or he hadn't made up his mind yet what he wanted to do. That was why she hadn't heard from him.

"Be good, boy," she said to Sparky. She locked the front door, ignored the bright sunlight, got in her car.

Barbara Norgaard's dilemma was a similar one, it occurred to her suddenly, as she waited at a red light. Faced with the knowledge that her husband was unfaithful, she hadn't known exactly what she wanted to do either—whether to take a stand and leave him, or to wait and think about it for a while. Twenty-some years was a long time to be married to someone. And the rage must have been tremendous. That and the feeling of betrayal. Just how great the rage, though?

170

The Farrell house was just south of the Westshore Lake Apartments, a large mock-Tudor with a three car garage and two Mercedes parked in the driveway. One for him and one for her, she thought as she pressed the bell.

There were no signs of the girl's parents; a maid answered the door and led Ellie back to the breakfast room where the thirteen-year-old was picking at the remnants of her breakfast. She smiled and spooned a bite of cantaloupe into her mouth.

"How was camp?" Ellie asked.

Quinn Farrell wrinkled her nose distastefully. "Same as it is every year," she replied. "Boring. But at least it's over and I'm back."

The maid fetched Ellie a cup of coffee, set out a silver sugar and cream service and retired through the swinging door to the kitchen.

"Parents still asleep?"

"Yup," she said carelessly. "My dad's taking me out to the stable, though, as soon as he gets up. I haven't seen Spartan Joe in over a week." She tossed her brown ponytail disapprovingly and turned large, coltish eyes on Ellie, looking for signs of commiseration. "That's too long to be away, don't you think? Especially with what's been happening out there while I've been gone. Poor Bart."

Ellie took a sip of coffee. "You liked Bart, did you?"

"Oh yes," she said, nodding her head emphatically. "I like him a lot. Imagine living like he does—all your worldly possessions small enough to fit into a cardboard box, moving somewhere different whenever you feel like it. He gets up when he wants to in the morning and goes to bed whenever he wants to at night. Nobody depends on him for anything. What a life! At least, what a life it was." She spooned another bite of cantaloupe into her mouth. "Do you suppose he'll be found guilty? Spend the rest of his life in jail?"

Ellie shook her head, said something about it being a little premature to be assuming that yet.

"Everybody else is glad, I bet," Quinn said. "He was always borrowing things without asking and pretending he worked his horses when he didn't. I don't even think Jerry liked him much, although he stuck up for him when Rich crabbed about him. And Barbara."

"Barbara, too, eh?"

Quinn nodded, grinned. "I always suspected she avoided the barn because of him, and I was right. Just before I had to go to that dumb camp I overheard her agreeing with Rich that he was bad for business. Rich was telling her about some bit of Jerry's that had disappeared, and she was looking all mad about it."

Ellie asked her if she'd ever seen anything that suggested Bart and Sue Anne were friends and she laughed. "You mean like boyfriend and girlfriend? Nope. Sue Anne didn't like Bart any better than anybody else did. She told me he was a loser, and he drank too much. Sue Anne was a jerk, though. I never listened to her."

A vacuum cleaner came to life down the hall, and she got up and shut the door facing that direction with the satisfied pronouncement that that ought to wake up her father.

My, she was tall for thirteen, Ellie thought.

"Want a roll?" the young girl asked. She moved a small bouquet of daisies off-center and shoved a plate of croissants at Ellie. Ellie took one, spread Danish butter and strawberry jam on it and ate it while, at her request, Quinn recalled what she could about the Salina show.

That was the one where Bart had let her have some beer, and she'd run into Rich and some girl coming out of her motel room. No. That had been in Iowa somewhere. It had been the weekend Barbara had put her on her old barrel horse, and she'd come in sixth, surprising both herself and the horse trainer's wife. No. Wait. She screwed up her face in concentration. Salina had been the one where she'd won the all-around trophy after getting two firsts and a second place in the youth events. Now she was nodding. The one where Bart had spent the weekend drunk, and Sue Anne had been particularly irritating, calling her a tomboy and suggesting she get lost. "All I did was ask her if I could sleep in her room that night instead of with Mrs. Johnson and her dog. I've got allergies and that dog drives me crazy. She shouldn't have had her dog there anyway. It said "no pets," right there in the room."

"But she said no?"

"That's right." Quinn looked at her innocently enough, but Ellie wondered. As precocious as she seemed, as ever-present at the stable as she had been, had she found out what was going on?

"What did Jerry Norgaard think of Sue Anne?"

The girl shrugged. "He always defends everybody," she said. "Gets this look on his face when he doesn't want to hear anymore and that's that. You clam up or he gets after you, makes you feel bad. I ought to know, I've spent enough time out there." She leaned her chin on her hand. "He's a great horse trainer, the best. Knows more than anybody about quarter horses and showing. When I grow up, I'm going to be one, too, unless, that is, my dad makes me be a doctor or a lawyer or something. Not that he can make me do anything I don't want to," she contradicted herself, her expression darkening.

"You know," she said after a pause, "sometimes I wish Jerry and Barbara were my parents. I could walk over and saddle my horse anytime I wanted to, and I'd have the benefit of years of experience. They'd have had me riding by the time I was three, maybe younger, knowing them." She grinned. "I don't like my real parents particularly. They bug me."

Were all teenagers that flippant, Ellie wondered, faintly recalling her envy of a friend's family during her teen years. Probably. "You get along well with Barbara I take it."

"We share a room at the shows when she comes," Quinn said happily. "She treats me kind of like the daughter she never had. Course she has Rich, but that's different. He's grown up and all, and he's a boy. I think Barbara wishes she'd grown to be as tall as me. I'm five foot seven. My real mom," she jerked her eyes skyward, "thinks I might grow another three inches which I kind of hope. It's good to have long legs when you train horses."

There was the sound of muffled footsteps in the hall and the door opened to reveal a handsome man in his mid-forties in robe and slippers, his expression first half-asleep, then startled when he caught sight of Ellie. Ellie recognized him from the funeral tape as Quinn's father.

"I thought I heard voices," he said awkwardly, adjusting his robe. "I assumed it was Maria and Quinn."

Ellie introduced herself, explaining that she'd had the visit okayed by his wife. "She told me to come by this morning after Quinn had a good night's sleep. I hope I haven't come too early."

"No problem, none whatsoever," he said. "She did mention it. I'd forgotten is all. I'm not quite awake yet." He rested his hands gently on his daughter's shoulders, and she rolled her eyes.

"We were just talking about Barbara Norgaard," Ellie said. "From what Quinn's been telling me, I gather you and your wife don't go to the horse shows with her."

Mr. Farrell, Martin, he insisted she call him, nodded his head easily. "Melanie and I don't know much about horses. When Quinn started begging us to buy her one, what? four years ago, a friend put me in touch with Jerry Norgaard, and he took care of everything. Picked out a horse for her, taught

**174**

her to ride and took her to the shows when he said she was ready. It was taken out of our hands which was okay by me since, as I. said, we didn't know anything about horses."

"It sounds like the Norgaards treat her like one of the family," Ellie said.

True, Martin agreed. They did, and he and his wife were thankful. "With all the drugs and peer pressure kids face to do crazy things these days, Quinn's better off spending her time at the stable, doing something wholesome," he said. "There's nothing she'd rather be doing and nothing, really, I can think of she'd be better off doing. For now, anyway."

During this conversation Maria, the maid, set another place at the table, brought in a fresh plate of croissants, and poured Martin Farrell a cup of steaming coffee. There were fresh raspberries and cream for him when he wanted them, she said. He'd rather see the paper, he said. All fluid motion, she disappeared, back in seconds with the *Sentinel.*

Ironic that the stable was embroiled in a murder investigation, and that the victim had done her share of drugs, Ellie thought, gesturing to Quinn that it was time to go before she got caught in a conversation with the father about Bart Vogel's arrest. Ironic too that everyone was ducking in and out of motel rooms with one another and getting too drunk to recall weekends at the horse shows, and yet he proclaimed the stable wholesome and a haven.

Quinn escorted Ellie to the front door. Ellie glanced back at Mr. Farrell in the breakfast room, his eyes glued to the front page of the paper, his face impassive. After the door closed behind her, she consulted her watch. What was Bieterman up to? Still hammering away at Vogel? She got into her car, looked in her notebook for a number, flipped out her phone, and dialed.

Howard Margolin picked up on the first ring. "We never went out on Friday nights," he said in response to her first question, sounding irritable. "Friday and Saturday nights are my biggest nights for business. Sue Anne would come sit at the bar with me, but that was it. No screwing around. Literally."

"Then you didn't spend weekend nights at her apartment?"

"No. I just told you. I'd stick around the lounge until two or so, then go home, to bed. We did our partying during the week when respectable folks were home watching prime time." He brayed. What'd she know about this Bart Vogel jerk, he asked after a pause.

Nothing, she said. Except she didn't think he did it. She hung up before he could respond, stared unseeingly at the shimmering pavement. She punched in another number.

"WBTV newsroom, Mitch Bassman speaking."

"Anything new on the Vogel thing?"

"Nope. I'm on my way over there now. Why? Where are you?"

"Never mind. Listen, can you do me a favor?"

After a pained sigh, he said he supposed he could.

"Get my notebook out of my desk. The one dated mid-June. Look up my notes with Bieterman."

In a few seconds he was back, pages rustling. "What a mess," he commented, and then, "crap, this goes on for ten pages. What do you want me to do, read every word?"

"Just give me the address of the pharmacy where the Cavanaugh woman bought the cigarettes."

There was more page rustling and finally he found it. "Wiltshire and 96th. God your handwriting is awful."

Ellie was about to hang up, make her getaway, when his voice, polite suddenly with a new hint of interest, stopped her. "What's up? You onto something?"

"No," she said. "Nothing really. Just thought I'd check out this one lead I never got around to before."

"Oh. Well." Now he sounded bored again, and impatient.

The phone clicked loudly in her ear.

# CHAPTER TWENTY-THREE

The manager of the Wiltshire Pharmacy, a spidery-looking older man who doubled as the store's druggist, looked wistful, a little crestfallen, when she explained who she was looking for. "He's at the register by the candy counter," he said. "Name's Barney," and directed her down a deserted aisle of antiseptics and bandages toward the back of the store.

"Mr. Sanborn was hoping you'd come with a prescription to fill," the college age looking Barney explained, tossing the magazine he'd been reading on the counter and standing up to reveal a height over six feet. "This isn't what you'd call a high volume traffic area out here what with the construction on 96th Street. We're hurting for business."

It had been difficult to get to with half the street torn up and one lonely flagman directing traffic, come to think of it. Barney explained they were supposed to be done with the job by the following week but then, they'd been hearing that all summer. He had a long face and a closely-shaved head; a swimmer or basketball player, Ellie decided.

His expression, when she explained she was a reporter working on the Cavanaugh case, changed from mild curiosity to keen interest. "You're kidding. Actually, the more I look at you, the more familiar you look. I'm sure I've seen you on television . . ."

Ellie couldn't help smiling, but then she got down to

business, asked the clerk if he'd been in the store when Sue Anne Cavanugh had come in the night of the murder.

She'd been in around seven-thirty, eightish, he said. "She stood around by the magazines for a while reading, then bought a pack of cigarettes, made a quick phone call, and left. That was about it. I told the police all of this after I saw a picture of her in the paper and read what happened. So what's the deal? I read in this morning's paper they arrested some cowboy for it. You know about that?"

"Not really," Ellie said vaguely. "Some friend of hers, I guess. Tell me more about this phone call. Could you hear anything she said? Get any idea of who she was speaking to or what she was talking about?"

Barney grinned, scratched his head. "She was irritated, that much I know for sure. I was sweeping up, tacking a few signs on the front window, too far away to hear much. But I did hear her swear a couple of times before she clicked off. Then she stomped out without a word. Got in a blue Mercedes and peeled out of here. I thought she'd plow right through the construction barricades but she didn't. Somehow she got through."

Ellie asked if he recalled anything else significant, and he shook his head. Only that the cigarettes she'd bought were Marlboro Gold Packs. But he didn't suppose she'd consider those facts significant. Ellie smiled, shook her head.

On her way out she stopped in the card section and picked out an anniversary card for her parents. "Noise must drive you crazy," she said to Mr. Sanborn over the cacophony of jackhammers outside. He put her card in a small sack. Noise he could take, he said with a mournful expression; it was the lack of business he was worried about.

Why had Sue Anne picked such an out-of-the-way spot to buy cigarettes, Ellie wondered as she pressed down on the accelerator at the flagman's prompting wave. Especially when

**179**

there were convenience stores and other pharmacies as close or closer to the Westshore Lake Apartments she could have reached with half the trouble.

Suddenly Ellie thought she knew why. She had come to meet someone, of course. Someone who had made this assignation and failed to show up. Ellie rolled up her window to escape the whirling dust and the noise of the jackhammers. She guided her car past the last barricade and rolled down her window to let the hot air in, the hotter air out. It was becoming clearer now. Childish? Could you call it that? In a way, she supposed. If you considered that the simple plan had worked.

The design on the girl's nails had changed. Ochre and chocolate plaid now instead of the lightning bolts, and there was no matching lighter.

Hunkered over a middle-aged woman's hands, Sylvia looked up with irritation, then smiled when she saw it was Ellie. "Thought you were my next customer, here early," she said. "Heard all about how the cops arrested that cowboy on the news last night. I never knew Sue Anne had such a valuable piece of jewelry. She never showed it to me. I mean, I knew Margolin bought her things and they were nice, but . . ."

She dropped her customer's hand, a woman she introduced as Mrs. Halperin, pulled out a cigarette and lit it. Ellie noted Mrs. Halperin looked mystified and faintly disapproving. "She never liked that guy Vogel," Sylvia said with conviction. "She thought he was a spook, I remember. 'He's a good-looker, Sylvia,' she said, 'but good looks don't pay the bills.' I wonder, did he drug her up and then kill her or what? Must have disliked her as much as she did him if he thought it was necessary to kill her and all. And why'd he kill her friend? She find all this out or something?"

**180**

She wasn't stoned today, that much was clear. With her mouth going like that it was more likely she'd snorted some cocaine, Ellie thought. Mrs. Halperin was listening now with open mouth. She'd caught the reference to murder.

"Will that detective be by again to take a statement from me? I suppose so. When you see him, tell him, remind him."

"Let's go in the back," Ellie said firmly.

Sylvia looked from Mrs. Halperin back to Ellie. "If Mrs. Halperin doesn't mind waiting?"

Mrs. Halperin looked like she would mind waiting; like she was trying desperately to recall who had sent her here in the first place, but she shook her head and sat back resignedly.

"Shirley Nardo," Ellie began when they were alone in the back room amid stacks of cardboard boxes, "was supplying Sue Anne with her drugs. The investigation has brought that out. But then you knew that before, didn't you. You sampled the goods. Smoked a little marijuana, tried some cocaine, whatever."

Sylvia tried to protest, but she silenced her. "I know why you didn't say anything. You were afraid it would get you in trouble; and you didn't feel right giving evidence against somebody you didn't know. But . . ." She skipped the part about how Sylvia also had been stoned, took a stab at what she hoped the manicurist could tell her. "What did Sue Anne say about Shirley Nardo?"

Sylvia began to pout. "What makes you think I know anything about that?"

Ellie got firmer. While she hadn't said anything too specific before, Sylvia should know she was working closely with the police on this case, she said. If Sylvia didn't want to level with her, fine, she'd call Det. Bieterman—perhaps she'd feel more comfortable giving her statement to him? She also mentioned withholding evidence . . .

**181**

Sylvia licked her lips and fluffed up her hair, looking indecisive. It was no big deal, she said finally, sullenly. Shirley'd taken them up to Sue Anne's apartment every once in a while; Sue Anne would sample the stuff; and she'd leave.

"Were you ever there when she made these deliveries of hers?"

"Just once . . . the last time." It had been a Friday night, she remembered, because her boyfriend had been ticked she'd been gone so long. He didn't approve of that kind of stuff, so of course she hadn't told him what she'd been doing. It was just that Sue Anne had begged her to come, told her she had to see her apartment, suggested she hadn't lived until she'd tried a little coke.

"The apartment was nice," she mumbled. "You ever been up there?" And then: "Shirley had somebody waiting for her outside, some guy, she said, and she was in a hurry. I don't know if you ever met her but she was pretty strung out . . . I got the impression Sue Anne didn't want her friend, the one in the car, in the apartment. She just paid Shirley and let her go."

"You didn't see him?"

"No. Like I said, she left." After that she and Sue Anne had tried out the stuff. Sylvia described an evening of alcohol and cocaine, a scary movie on Netflicks—some bloody thing about a man with a chainsaw—and an angry boyfriend waiting up for her when she got home.

"But you didn't see Shirley leave. Didn't see this guy she was with?"

"No. I told you I didn't."

Ellie studied her round face intently and decided this time she had told her the truth. At least what she remembered.

"Anything else you'd like to add?"

Sylvia shook her head. "My boyfriend better never hear

**182**

about this . . . he'd kill me."

Ellie remained expressionless and stood to go. The front of the shop was empty. There was a check by the cash register and the faint scent of some cloying perfume, but no sign of Mrs. Halperin.

Ellie avoided Sylvia's accusing expression. She let herself out.

Bobby Hunsacker had lied. At least she was fairly sure he had.

He recoiled at first, no doubt unnerved when Shirley came into view. Eerie it was, he said, seeing Shirley alive. He wiped at his nose.

Ellie adjusted the focus a little, and they both watched as the young woman strode by, a downward slant to her lips. She resembled her mother, Ellie saw now: both mother and daughter had the hollow-boned structure of birds, both looked wasted, but Shirley had the advantage of animation, something Ellie sensed her mother may never have had.

It was from footage at the gravesite that Hunsacker made his identification. "Can you stop the thing?" he asked as the camera traveled through the crowd.

"Just tell me when . . ."

"Now," he said, staring intently at the screen. He pointed with a shaking hand. "No question," he said. "Parked next to me in the lot, walked right by her when she was coming out."

Ellie froze the screen on that shot and the two of them stared at the monitor for a few seconds. Finally, Ellie switched the thing off. Wordlessly the two of them left the television station, and a short time later Ellie dropped the kid off on the corner by his apartment building. He'd confessed to lying about being with Shirley when she'd delivered some drugs to Sue Anne's apartment rather sullenly. He hadn't actually gotten out of the car or gone in, was his excuse.

A few blocks away she pulled over and put in a call to Bieterman. He didn't pick up. It was early evening now and she had the day off. No time to wait to hear from him. She sat in her car for a few minutes thinking, flipped open her notebook, and punched in another call. This time someone picked up.

# CHAPTER TWENTY-FOUR

Was there anything to this ESP? Could the messages she was getting today be an indication she had perceptive powers, Quinn wondered as she swapped absently at a horsefly on Spartan Joe's neck.

She reined the animal through the gate and fastened it behind her, taking care to be sure the latch caught properly. She had been so relieved earlier, not exactly happy, but relieved. Bart had been arrested, the search was over as far as the police were concerned, and things could get back to normal. But now?

It was getting late and she really ought to get back to the barn. Why did this feeling, this worry, have to hit now, just when she'd thought it was all over, she had nothing more to worry about? She reined the animal to a halt, sat quietly in the still oppressive heat thinking.

A lot of it was because of that reporter. She wasn't convinced it was Bart. She was out there, nosing around, finding out what? And then there was Jerry, himself. He'd acted like she was a thorn in his side this morning, answering her questions in monosyllables and then going back to the house. A little flicker of worry pinched her nose, flaring her nostrils. If only she hadn't found out what she did, sat back for so long doing nothing about it.

Had the reporter suspected? If she did, she hadn't let on.

**185**

But then, she wouldn't have, Quinn reasoned. She would have felt Quinn was too young to discuss such matters with, too innocent, naive. She scoffed. "Little does she know, huh Joe?" she crooned, leaning forward in the stirrups so she could wrap her thin arms around the horse's neck.

The animal dropped its head and cropped at a stubble of wild grass, then grasped an ear of corn in its strong teeth and yanked hard, almost unseating her. Quinn gathered up the reins and pulled up his head. "Do you think she knows?" Quinn asked him, worried now, but he paid no attention, busy trying to eat the vegetable with a bit in his mouth.

"I wish," she said calmly, quietly, "she'd give it up. Forget about it." But the worry that she wouldn't kept bubbling up, spoiling the serenity of her ride, making her angry and more than a little apprehensive.

She'd had no choice, that was for sure. People had to make up their minds about things and then, once that was accomplished, remain resolute, true to course. Loyalty, that's what it all boiled down to. Otherwise things got too chaotic, too unpredictable. Even though she had this feeling, this crushing doubt, she wouldn't change her mind. She couldn't. Bart, in addition to his slothfulness, had proven a fool. That was how she was going to look at it.

Quinn shrugged off the horse's back. She sat on a fallen log and let the horse graze at her feet. Maybe she ought to have stayed at camp, looked at it as a haven, instead of a punishment. At least there she'd been removed from all of this, hadn't had to think about it so much, worry about it. Quinn pet Spartan Joe absently and wondered what she was going to do. What could she do?

Jerry Norgaard moved slowly down the aisle dumping a scoop of grain in each feed trough from the wheelbarrow he pushed in front of him. He took no notice when a horse laid back its ears at him or cribbed nervously on the wooden bin.

L'Heureux, up in the loft raking loose wisps of hay into piles, had just finished dropping flakes of it to the horses below, and he gazed down now at the grey horse's back through the feeding window. The horse munched contentedly.

"Put me on the filly tomorrow?" he asked unexpectedly, bringing Jerry out of his trance.

"We'll see, son. We'll see. I don't know."

Rich frowned slightly, then swung around and clambered down the ladder. "You talk to Margolin about his horses yet?"

Jerry nodded and dumped another container of grain into a feed trough. "He called me last night. Wants me to sell them for whatever I can get."

L'Heureux pulled a coil of hose off its holder and stuck it in the nearest water bucket. With that attitude, he wouldn't get much. "He say anything about Vogel?"

As a matter-of-fact he had, plenty, but Jerry didn't have the strength to repeat it. "He was surprised, I think," was all he said. Surprised. Everyone's initial reaction had been that, or something like it. Quinn Farrell had dogged him all morning asking questions, 'weren't you shocked when you heard?' 'what do you think will happen now?' 'did you think Bart would do such a thing?' until he'd had to go back to the house to get away from her.

And earlier than that, he'd heard from Greta Johnson. Normally making her appearance around ten, she'd interrupted Barbara and his silent breakfast that morning to register her opinion.

"Scares the pants off me to think he's been around all these months, scoping us out," she'd said after telling them how dumbfounded she'd been at the news. "What if one of us had found those pearls or something? Why, he might have strangled one of us." Barbara had gotten up to get her a cup

**187**

of coffee, and he'd excused himself. Perhaps he'd appeared rude, but he was beyond appearances. That woman was the last person on earth he felt compelled to discuss Bart Vogel with.

And then Barbara. If anything, she'd been conspicuous by her silence. That and the grim look she harbored.

He'd been late for supper the night before, but, perhaps accustomed to it, she'd said nothing. They'd eaten in silence and after he'd carried his plate to the sink, gone to the den, he heard her doing up the pots and pans. Taking, he thought, her time about it. Later she'd come in, switched on the television set. Again, not a word.

This silence had been coming on for some time, he realized now, only he'd been too upset to notice. She had grown very quiet, had become engrossed in her gardening, had had little to say to him for some time.

Margolin's call had been almost a relief. "That son of a bitch ought to be glad they've got him in jail," he'd said darkly when Jerry picked up the receiver. Barbara had looked up, then back at the set when he'd assumed an offhand manner.

Margolin described in graphic detail what he'd do to Vogel if the police ever made the mistake of letting him out. And later, "You know the creep was such a cold s.o.b. he could kill just like that?"

No, he hadn't, he'd said. Bart had never shown a vicious side; if anything he was more like a kid, a kid who refused to grow up. Of course he hadn't said that. What he wanted to say was he didn't do it, but he kept silent, shook his head when Margolin snorted, let out another expletive.

"I'm not shocked," L'Heureux said now, startling him out of his dark thoughts. "The only thing that does surprise me is it didn't occur to us to suspect him earlier. I mean, here we had equipment disappearing right before our eyes, we knew he abused horses in Oklahoma . . ."

''The police still aren't sure he's the one . . . ''

"Well, they will be. Of course he did it . . . "

The two of them finished their chores to the strains of pop tunes from the radio and an occasional snort or whinny from one of the horses. When L'Heureux had started up his truck and driven off with a casual wave of his hand, Jerry stumped back through the barn and went into his office.

This was the time of day he'd always appreciated most, with chores done and nothing more expected of him, but now that thought didn't occur to him. He picked up a paper clip, bent it until it finally snapped, then slumped back in his chair. All of this was his fault, all of it, he thought miserably. And there was nothing, really, he could do about it.

He took off his cap and tossed it on the desk. There was no way out, he decided, after he'd taken that first irrevocable step. He should have known that. And not owning up to finding the key had been a mistake, he could see that now. Better to establish a certain trust with the police. They probably knew now that he had it back.

Barbara, he thought in despair. What's happened? Why did it have to go so far? He wondered idly about that phone call from the reporter. Her questions made no sense.

Back at the house, she pulled a warmed-over casserole out of the oven and set it on the counter.

He'd be late again, she thought listlessly. Back before all of this she could have set a timer, had dinner hot on the table ten minutes after Rich drove by; Jerry'd been that prompt. But now . . . now it was seven, eight o'clock sometimes before he came in, washed his hands, sat silently, staring at his food.

She'd have a drink, she decided impulsively. Wasn't there a bottle of wine in the cabinet over the refrigerator? Something to settle her nerves and give her courage for what she had to do. She dragged a stool over, found the bottle in the back, and poured herself a generous glass.

Neither of them drank much and the alcohol went immediately to her head. She had been one for beer back in the days she'd been with Bart and his friends. Only Jerry hadn't been much for it, and she'd quit under his disapproving eye. Stodgy, that's what he was. Or had been . . . Cradling the wine glass to her chest, she wandered through the central hallway toward the den, catching sight of herself in the old beveled mirror over the hall table. Dark circles ringed her eyes, and there was an unhealthy pallor to her complexion. She brushed back a limp tendril and turned away.

The den was small, close, and she opened the shutters to get rid of that feeling. No one in sight. She'd hoped to see Jerry's familiar frame shuffling toward her down the lane. Maybe he'd stay there all night, she thought, sinking into a chair. Maybe he sensed what was ahead and hoped to avoid it for a while. But it had to be done. If Jerry wasn't going to do it, and clearly he had shown no inclination so far, she'd have to be the catalyst, galvanize him into action.

She took another sip of the wine and admired the shimmering prisms the crystal cast on the carpet. It tasted brackish, the wine did. A quarter horse magazine lay face-down on his chair, and she picked it up, put it on top of the pile stacked by the wall. He wouldn't throw them out, stubbornly maintaining that one day reference to an article in one or another of them might prove handy. A few years ago, angry, she'd called the library, offered the librarian the entire collection, Jerry-be-damned, but the woman wasn't interested. Everything was digitalized now, and they simply didn't have the room for paper copies. Now piles of them grew like mushrooms in odd corners.

The thought occurred to her to carry them out to the front yard and set fire to them. Get rid of them all once and for all. Send up a flame that could be seen for miles around. For a split second the impulse was almost strong enough, but then, no, that would be childish, she decided. She took another sip of her wine.

Perhaps it hadn't been such a good idea, drinking. Or, perhaps what she needed was a little more, say one more glass. She might as well get rid of the stuff. Resettled in her chair with another one, only half-full this time—all she could get out of the bottle—she felt her resolution grow, inhibitions and fears forgotten. There was no looking back. It would be done, and tonight. She closed her eyes and felt a peacefulness settle over her, a feeling she hadn't experienced for a long time. Jerry found her that way, asleep in the chair, when he came in.

# CHAPTER TWENTY-FIVE

Ellie pulled into her driveway just as her phone rang. Bieterman. Finally. She sat in her car while she updated him. Told him what she suspected had actually happened, what the kid, Bobby, had said. What the only conclusion could be.

Sit tight, he said when she finished. He'd take it from there. And he clicked off.

The porch light was burning, lights blazing in the living room and dining room. Exhausted from her efforts, relieved that she'd finally connected with Bieterman, she clicked off herself and went inside. Sparky greeted her at the door.

What would Bieterman do with what she'd told him, she wondered. Would he make an arrest? Get a warrant? In what order if he did? Part of her wished she could be in on the action, but the prudent part told her she'd done plenty and now she needed to take a back seat.

She made some toast, turned on the coffee maker, and sat down at the kitchen table, Sparky curling happily at her feet. An hour went by. She thought about trying to call Bieterman again, but then she decided that wasn't a good idea. She'd just have to wait; not her strong suit. He was the cop, he was the one with the resources to take it from here, and she needed to—as he said—sit tight.

But it wasn't easy. She got up from the table, walked

around in her silent house and checked her answering machine; no messages, no blinking light. She peered out the living room window at the darkened front yard as a car's taillights receded in the distance. It was getting very late and things were pretty much settled for the night except for the occasional late nighter heading home from somewhere, or maybe heading to work on a late shift. It occurred to her that she'd never brought the paper in that morning, and she decided to get it off the porch, read a while. But when she stepped outside, the damn thing wasn't on the porch. Or the steps. Ellie, barefoot, descended the steps, noted the cool grass at her feet and went into the yard in search of the paper. By the light of the porch, she spied it finally in the straggly half-dead bushes that flanked the edge of her yard.

She made her way over to the bushes as Sparky barked from inside the house, a loud yap, and then another. How had she managed to leave him inside, she wondered just as someone stepped out of the shadows.

"Hello Ellie," he said.

Goosebumps rose on her arms, and her scalp tingled. Ellie could make him out in the dim light. He wore his customary cap, his jeans, crepe-soled shoes. His usually benign face was tense now, his voice deliberate. "Should have left things alone, you know. Let the police handle things and stayed out of it. It's too bad."

He took a step toward her, and Ellie cleared her throat.

"That wouldn't have been fair to Vogel," she said timorously, her voice sounding thin and high. And afraid.

He shook his head, took another step toward her. "Fair? What's fair? Ten years I've groveled out at that stable, shoveled shit, waited for him to teach me about the horses, told myself it was worth it, someday it would be mine. And then I find out he's messing around with Sue Anne Cavanaugh."

He laughed humorlessly. "What was I supposed to do?

**193**

Sit there and watch everything fall apart before my eyes?"

Rich L'Heureux, the stable hand the Norgaards considered almost family, scowled. He didn't know how to train, and neither did Barbara. There was a big difference between riding barrel racers once and breaking and training horses. No way could he and Barbara have handled it if Jerry had skipped out with the Cavanaugh woman. "Jerry had to stick around" he said simply. "Farmland isn't worth anything right now, and the place is only valuable because of him."

He had her by the arm now and was prodding her back toward the porch and the house. His breathing was rapid, more like panting, and Ellie imagined she was staring into the eyes of a big cat. Had Shirley Nardo seen him in her rear view mirror like this before he pounced? Perhaps caught a glimpse of him while they struggled?

It had all been there on the tape. Shirley making her snide comment about Margolin, him flushing, the Norgaards and L'Heureux looking startled. It was only after she'd pieced it together that Ellie'd seen more than mere surprise on L'Heureux's face.

A flicker of recognition, a second of panic. He'd had no choice, she'd realized as she and that Bobby kid played the tape, backed it up, viewed it again in slow motion. It was only a matter of time before Shirley'd made the connection, figured out she'd seen him there, sitting in his truck, observing the apartment building. There'd been a puzzled expression on her face at the funeral . . .

He licked his lips. "It's too bad you couldn't stay out of it. I kind of liked you."

They had reached the steps now and she thought briefly about trying to run away. She was going to be trapped once they went in the house and he shut the door. She faked a stumble in an effort to loosen his hold on her, but he wasn't surprised and his grip merely tightened.

"What makes you think you're going to get away with this?" she asked. "With Bart in jail, they'll know they've got the wrong man."

He frowned. "Like I said, I have no choice. I'm going to make it look like you surprised a burglar, tried to stop him . . ."

Now he spied Sparky on the other side of the door, wanting to come out. He paused for a split second, then opened the door and pushed her inside, never relaxing his steel-like grip. Sparky backed out of the way, and wagged his tail at Ellie. Poor dog. How was he to know this man represented danger, she thought resignedly. She was in the house and with or without a companion, Sparky didn't care. She was back and he was happy.

Rich seemed a little unsettled with the dog nonetheless. Would the dog come at him? Ellie could tell he was deliberating about what to do with Sparky. Suddenly he lunged at the black and white animal, grabbed him by the collar and maneuvered both Ellie and the dog to the nearest door— it led to the basement—opened it, kicked the unsuspecting dog down the steps and slammed it.

Ellie had her opportunity. Right when he slammed the door, his grip on Ellie's arm loosened for a second. She snaked out of his grasp and headed down the darkened hall to the bathroom—the only room that had a door that locked. She raced inside, slammed the door and turned the key just as he crashed into it full-bore. Frantically, Ellie searched her pockets for her cell phone. Not there.

Now he was kicking the door with all his might. Thank god the house was an old one and the door was solid. It would hold—at least for a while.

Ellie looked around the bathroom. She eyed the only window in the room: a small, high, frosted one. Even if she could get up to it, it was too little; she couldn't get out that way. Well, if she couldn't get out, what could she use to defend herself? She cast around for a weapon and her eyes focussed on a small pair of scissors on the side of the sink. With one stride she was there and had them in her hand. She turned back to the door, arm raised defensively.

Another massive blast as he kicked the door with all his might. The wood may hold, but Ellie doubted the lock itself could withstand much more. She crept over to the light switch and shut off the light. Now, when he got in—and she was pretty sure he would—he wouldn't be able to see her right away, she reasoned. That split second might allow her to get by him and out. Might. She angled her body to the left of the door, visualizing him charging inside, her stepping behind him and away.

She stood taut, every nerve on edge. And then, suddenly, the blasts stopped. She waited a few seconds and listened intently. Nothing. Not a sound. Where the hell was he? What was he doing? For some odd reason, the silence was more unnerving than the kicking of the door. At least then she'd known where he was and what he was up to.

She put her ear up against the wall and listened intently. Now she heard faint sounds coming from the kitchen. First a drawer being opened and closed, then a cupboard. He was looking for something. What? A tool to pry open the lock?

Ellie decided now was her one opportunity to escape. If she stayed here, eventually he'd get in, and the odds of her slipping by him weren't that great. This way, at least she'd have a better chance of running past him and out the front door. Quietly, she unlocked the bathroom door and eased it open. The hallway was dark and she could still hear noises as he searched in the kitchen. She stepped cautiously over the door frame and into the hall and began inching her way down the hall towards him. He had turned on an under cabinet fluorescent light in the kitchen that faintly lit the hall, and she could see the basement door to her right. Nervously, she extended the scissors in her left hand and continued to inch down the hall. All she had to do was pass the kitchen in order to get to the living room and the front door. She took a few more muffled steps, eyes peeled on the kitchen doorway.

She was just passing the basement door when he stepped quietly into view. "Thought I heard you," he said in a low voice.

Ellie, not sure why, did the first thing that occurred to her—grabbed the basement door knob and flung it open. Whatever her intentions—put a barrier between them; run downstairs to get away from him—two things happened almost simultaneously. First Rich froze for a second and then Sparky erupted from the basement, teeth bared and growling low in his throat.

Sparky went straight for Rich, springing at him full force. He sank his teeth into the man's arm and the two of them began to circle around as Rich tried to shake Sparky off. Without further thought, Ellie grabbed her cell phone lying on the table by the door and ran outside into the dark front yard. She heard a loud yelp and was afraid what that meant but she continued out of the yard and down the street without a backward glance. Street lights lit up the road. She'd be too visible, she decided. She veered into the next door neighbor's darkened yard, crawled under a tangled snarl of bushes, and caught her breath before she whipped out her cell phone and called Bieterman.

It rang two, three, four times. Suddenly she sensed, rather than saw L'Heureux outside, coming her way. Whether he could see her or not, she wasn't sure. He was cradling the arm Sparky'd clamped down on, but his walk was deliberate and his approach deathly quiet.

Ellie closed her eyes and froze. Tried not to breathe.

Now she imagined she could hear him, shoes padding

softly on the grass, getting closer. She dared to open her eyes and saw that he was on the sidewalk, peering intently into the yard where she was hidden. She closed her eyes again and tried not to breathe, while simultaneously silencing her cell phone so there would be no light or noise from it to betray her. Fortunately, no porch light shone here to help him; the yard was dark except for the street light shining faintly from the corner. A slight breeze rifled the leaves of a tree overhead, and then a far off train let out a plaintive whistle.

She felt for her scissors. Yes, she still had them. That comforted her slightly.

L'Heureux coughed now and put his hand to his mouth. He started walking again, took a few steps toward the neighbor's driveway. Stopped. Listened. To Ellie, it looked like he was staring right at her now. But he couldn't be or he'd be after her, she thought. Don't move. Now he swore softly, and it was obvious by the way he sounded that he was in pain. So Sparky had hurt him. Good. She didn't let herself think what he might have done to the dog.

How much closer should she let him get before she ran?

And then he did an odd thing. He started walking toward the back yard. Up the neighbor's driveway and around the house. Away from her instead of toward her. Ellie didn't know what to make of this. Had he heard something back there behind the house? What should she do? Stay here under the bushes or run? If she chose to run, run where? She could see her car parked on her driveway but she knew she didn't have her keys with her. Maybe she should sneak back into her house and lock the door? Or was this just a ploy from Rich to flush her out—would she be wiser to stay where she was? The train whistled again, closer this time. Ellie kept her head down, willing herself not to panic and to make the right decision.

And then a twig snapped and the decision was made for

**198**

her. Ellie saw shoes, long legs and then his face as he approached her in the dark. He had a sly, intent look, and again she was reminded of a cat stalking its prey.

Adrenaline surged and she leaped to her feet and started running. She was barefoot and the burned-out stubble felt brittle, but she didn't pause—she ran as fast as she'd ever run, toward her own house and the front door and the lock that would protect her from this relentless guy.

And somehow she made it. Twisted and turned as he lunged for her and kept running full bore, dropped the scissors in her haste but slammed and locked the door just as he almost got her, his eyes half-closed and his breath on her neck. She leaned back against the door, gasping and tried to catch her breath. What now? WHAT NOW?

She pulled out her cell phone and raced for the kitchen and a weapon. A knife? Sparky lay in the hallway, not moving. She almost tripped over him in her haste. Oh my god, she thought. But she didn't drop down on her knees to see if the prostrate creature was still alive. That would have to come later, if there was a later. In the kitchen she jerked open a drawer, scrabbled frantically for a knife. Her fingers closed around a steak knife and she yanked it out, set it on the counter and clicked her cell phone on again, dialed Bieterman. Pick up, she prayed. Pick up. It rang once, twice.

And then out of the corner of her eye she saw Rich staring at her from outside through the kitchen door. He was smiling faintly, and he had a large rock in his hand. He took a swing at the pane in the door and glass shattered everywhere. Now he stuck his hand inside the hole and was groping for the doorknob. Ellie scooped up the knife, ran to the door, and began slashing his hand blindly. Blood spurt and he howled furiously. Now she stuck the knife into his palm and with an even louder howl he jerked his hand free of the shattered glass.

Suddenly, through a blur she heard the front door pop open. What the—? The house fill with policemen, guns drawn.

"You all right?" Bieterman yelled at her as four uniformed cops burst into the kitchen, closed in on L'Heureux on the other side of the door, guns drawn.

"Barely," she said, and sat down, hard. She caught a glimpse of Rich's face—shocked, disbelieving—before he disappeared into the blue melee, then closed her eyes and waited for the room to stop spinning.

"Well," she said, and then again, "well." Then, speechless, she drew silent.

# CHAPTER TWENTY-SIX

"The stable hand," Tom Hancock said over the din at Branigans. "What put you onto him? I don't remember hearing much about him before." She had just finished telling him about the events leading up to L'Heureux's capture the night before . . .

Ellie munched on popcorn and tried to remember the scenario of events that led her to suspect L'Heureux could be the murderer. "It was a series of things," she said slowly. He'd always been a possibility, but she didn't consider him the one until she'd eliminated the Norgaards as suspects. Then it was obvious. "It started to look like someone was framing Bart Vogel," she said. "There were three people I considered who might have had reason to do that. Barbara Norgaard, Jerry Norgaard, and L'Heureux. When I'd decided in my own mind that the Norgaards had other reasons for their actions, I knew it was L'Heureux. He made it a point to attack Vogel every time I talked to him, sometimes subtly, sometimes not . . . "

"And why did he do that?"

"Vogel treated him like a farmhand. Made fun of him, teased him about not being much of a rider. Of course, who knows? Maybe L'Heureux started it, said something or did something to Vogel first. It doesn't really matter. All I know is L'Heureux despised him. When he decided he had to kill Sue

Anne, and he overheard Vogel and Davis planning to steal the pearls, Vogel became his scapegoat. It was really quite simple. Childish."

Hancock took a sip of his beer, leaned back in his seat. "Pretty incredible," he said. He'd caught a glimpse of the freckled stable hand as the police hustled him by a group of photographers in front of police headquarters earlier. "He didn't look the part."

"He didn't, did he," Ellie agreed, shivering a little at the image of him coming at her the night before.

"What about the Norgaards? How did they take the news?"

Bieterman, that afternoon, had told Ellie about his meeting with the Norgaards: Barbara Norgaard had required medication to calm her down, Norgaard had been rendered merely speechless. She frowned. "It hasn't been easy. L'Heureux was like a son to them, you know." Each had suspected the other, she explained. Barbara Norgaard was convinced her husband had done it because she thought Sue Anne was blackmailing him; Norgaard thought his wife had found out about his affair and in a rage killed her herself, then pinned the thing on Bart Vogel. They didn't realize both were wrong until the night before when the wife confronted the husband and demanded they talk the thing over.

"Could have saved themselves a lot of trouble if they'd done that earlier," Hancock said.

"L'Heureux must have been quite the actor," Ellie said. "Convincing them all these years he cared about them when really all he wanted was their money."

"Maybe it didn't start out that way," Hancock said. "Maybe the money got to be more important as he got older. Who knows?"

Ellie shrugged. Bieterman's men had found stacks of overdue bills in L'Heureux's apartment in Milvern in addition to several of Jerry Norgaard's bridles. He had stolen them to focus suspicion on Bart Vogel, they had concluded.

"So tell me," Hancock said. "If he planned the thing so carefully, why'd he go there without a key. Didn't he know where it was?"

Yes, Ellie said. He knew where it was. But all along he'd worried that Vogel would screw up or get drunk and chicken out on his burglary plans if things got too difficult, so he let Vogel discover and take the key. "He did have a bit of a scare that night when he phoned Sue Anne's apartment and she was home instead of at the lounge with Margolin like he'd counted on. He had to get her out of there quick so Vogel could go in and burgle the place. That's why he asked her to meet him at the pharmacy under the pretext he had something to tell her about Norgaard. Then, when she phoned him, mad, he said he'd be by later. He ended up having to pound on the door only because she got so stoned and drunk she passed out."

Hancock considered that. "And the other girl, Shirley Nardo, why did he kill her?"

Ellie told him about Bobby Hunsacker, how it had turned out he'd been with Nardo one night, had stayed in her car while she'd delivered Sue Anne some drugs in her apartment. How Nardo had walked right by L'Heureux in the parking lot. How on the videotape of Sue Anne's funeral she'd noticed a reaction from him when he saw Nardo. "He was afraid she'd mention having seeing him at the apartment building to the cops. He decided he couldn't take a chance on her connecting him to Sue Anne so he killed her." She sniffed. "Bobby Hunsacker was sitting in Nardo's car when she walked by. He saw him, too. Only L'Heureux didn't see him. Luckily for him."

He let out a low whistle. "Talk about luck. What was L'Heureux doing there that night? Reconnoitering?"

"Yes." And then: "Remember the thirteen-year-old I told you about, Quinn Farrell?" And at his nod: "She told Bieterman this afternoon she was worried all along Bart hadn't done it, but she thought Norgaard had so she kept quiet." She'd idolized him, it seemed. Norgaard, she had discovered one night when she'd come out late to work her horse, was kissing Sue Anne in the tack room. Quinn had slipped out unseen but been tortured over it—she thought of Barbara and Jerry as second parents. After Bart had been arrested, she'd tried to convince herself to forget about it, but one look at Norgaard on her return from camp had told her the police had the wrong man—and Norgaard knew it. Bieterman told her the young girl seemed vastly relieved at the news: she'd never particularly cared about L'Heureux one way or the other.

Several reporters came over to their table now to congratulate Ellie on her work in the investigation. "You went a little above and beyond, didn't you?" one of them jested.

"Say, I heard something about your dog?" someone else prodded.

Ellie nodded soberly. She flashed back to the night before, saw herself as if in a dream, suddenly coming out of her confusion, remembering Sparky, running around the corner and dropping down on her knees to stare intently at the black and white dog sprawled out in the hallway. Was he breathing? She put her head to his chest and heard faint signs that he was. Out of the corner of her eye, she saw the large pliers she kept in the kitchen junk drawer laying there beside the dog. She'd grabbed him up in her arms and shot out the door, ignoring protestations from Bieterman about leaving, laid him gently on her passenger seat and sped to an all-night vet clinic a couple of miles away. A gentle woman vet had taken him away, come back twenty minutes later with the news that he had a skull fracture and they'd have to wait and see. So Rich had hit him on the head with her pliers—pliers he'd intended to use on the lock of the bathroom door.

She'd been calling the clinic almost hourly ever since and finally received more hopeful news. His spells of consciousness were becoming more frequent. "It's going to take a while to know for sure, but I have my fingers crossed," she said. It occurred to her now as she looked around at the group of reporters nodding and smiling encouragingly, that Sparky had saved her life there at a very critical point during her ordeal. So they were equal now, she and Sparky—both had come through for the other at an almost fatal juncture in the other's life. She felt a warm gratitude to the dog and smiled faintly. But she didn't tell anyone circled around her this. Sparky's background and how he'd come into her life was a secret she wouldn't share with any of her friends, even her family. Next thing you knew someone was telling someone else about it and then someone was letting slip to someone else who intentionally or not, was telling someone like say Bieterman who—whether he was sympathetic or not— would be uncomfortable with the illegality of it all.

"You know, it didn't work out like I expected," Ellie said to Hancock after the group of journalists had finished with their questions and drifted away. "Remember in journalism school being taught how I.F. Stone described his feelings as a cub reporter?"

Hancock shook his head.

"He was covering a fire. Something about how it was so much fun he ought to have been arrested. 'I was like a small boy,' he said, 'covering a hell of a big fire . . . it was wonderful, exciting . . . God had given this to me. And I forgot—that it's really burning.' Well, that's how I felt about this case," she mused. "It was wonderful, exciting, until Rich came to my house to kill me. Then it got real. So did the murders."

Hancock was silent. After a while Ellie drained her beer,

said she thought it was time to go home. He walked her out to her car. If she was afraid, he could come over . . .

Ellie smiled. Not tonight, she said. Some other time.

What, she wondered, as she coasted past the silent, dark homes in her neighborhood, would it be like to work from two p.m. to ten? To get off work at a more reasonable hour and have a social life again?

"Ellie," Fred Burrows had said, taking her into his office that afternoon and closing the door while the other newsroom occupants eyed them curiously through the glass walls, "I don't want to say I approve of your methods, but . . ." and he'd shifted her, just like that, off the night shift.

What about late night, she'd asked before she thought. Who was going to cover that time slot if he was moving her up?

"I've hired another reporter," he said. "A woman. Writes well. You can work with her on her videos some. Your times overlap enough." That had brought Mitch to mind. Now she'd be working three hours a day with Mitch. Could she bear it?

"You and he do a fair job together," Burrows said. "I want you to continue to pair up whenever possible."

She'd sleep until noon, she decided, as she coasted into her driveway. Unplug her phone, turn off her cell, disconnect her recorder, try to catch up on days of no sleep.

A ringing phone greeted her when she opened the door. She'd already talked to her parents once, endured her mother's hysterics, her father's not so veiled hints that maybe she hadn't ought to have been so involved. Who else would be calling who didn't know her cell phone number?

It was Margolin, calling to thank her. "I've been trying to catch you all day . . ." Ellie listened for a while, tried to interject that Bieterman and Morrison deserved some credit but he'd have none of it. "They were itching to nail me," he said in his gruff voice. "If it weren't for you . . . "

There was nothing for it but to accept his praise, promise him she'd bring a friend by his restaurant for a free meal, soon. Bieterman, she thought tiredly as she retrieved the mail. She'd bring Bieterman. If he'd come. That would frost Margolin . . .

The envelope was under a pile of circulars, advertisements, a couple of bills. Ellie almost chucked it out with the rest of the junk.

It was from Gordon.

*Dear Ellie,* it began. *This is hard for me to write* . . . Several paragraphs were devoted to his loneliness, his unhappiness, his fears; Ellie scanned them quickly. *You may have suspected something more than friendship developing between Sonya Phillips (the graduate assistant I mentioned) and me. I'll spare you the details. Suffice it to say she was here, and you were there . . .*

Ellie looked up, then continued reading.

*I want you to know that I'm in the process of trying to decide just what my feelings are at this stage. Sonya is a wonderful woman, but I find myself posing the following questions: Did we find one another for the right reasons? Have I leaped into a new relationship too soon? Am I being fair to you? I do miss you, you see. It occurs to me now, I need to be pushed. I am, on occasion, too passive . . . And the last two years with you can't be dismissed easily.*

Several lines developed how he'd anguished over his dilemma and then: *I don't know what the outcome of all this will be, how you'll react, what I'll decide. But I want you to know you still mean a lot to me . . . I'll be back in August to visit my parents and want to talk to you then.*

She crumbled up the letter and tossed it on the table.

She didn't feel as badly as she'd thought she would, she decided after a few minutes reflection. After all she'd kind of suspected the worst for a while.

She went over to the window and watched Mr. Dinsmore next door as he straggled past his living room window in a sweaty undershirt, a can of beer in his hand.

Yes, she supposed she could be a little pushy. If you wanted to call it that. To be more accurate, she was someone who worked single-mindedly to get what she wanted. She'd always been that way. And she'd seen what she thought Gordon should want and set him off in that direction. If that meant she'd emasculated Gordon, and she kind of thought she might have, so be it. Maybe they weren't good for each other—or maybe she was good for him but he wasn't good for her. Foremost in her mind right now was succeeding at work. She might even concede that she was getting obsessed about it.

She saw Bieterman sitting on her couch earlier that afternoon, explaining how he and his men had shown up at her house the night before. "Your phone call got us on the move. Morrison and I immediately headed out to look around for L'Heureux after I told you to sit tight. We went by his apartment, the stable, drove by some bars in the area, no Rich. And then I got a call from you on my cell. Actually, just a couple of rings. You weren't there when I picked up."

That would have been when she was hiding in the bushes, Ellie explained soberly. She'd had to disconnect the call and turn off the ringer for fear it would lead L'Heureux to her hiding place.

"Which explains now why, when I called you back, you didn't pick up," Bieterman said, nodding thoughtfully. "Well, anyway, we headed straight for your house after that call and radioed for backup on the way. It was just too late to get a casual call from you, we figured. You had to be in trouble."

"And then I tried to call you again from the kitchen and had to hang up."

Bieterman nodded grimly. "By that time we were almost there."

"Thank god."

They looked at one another, the swarthy, intense-faced Bieterman with an unfathomable expression—anger? fear?— Ellie with a look of gratitude she didn't try to suppress. She couldn't imagine what would have happened if the police hadn't arrived when they did. She didn't want to imagine . . . although she left this unsaid.

He'd left pretty soon after that. He had a meeting with his Captain about something, then an appointment with an assistant D.A., then he and Morrison were questioning a couple of witnesses in a new case they'd just started working on . . .

Bieterman was a kindred spirit, she thought now. Work was everything to him. Moreover, she doubted he could be bossed around.

She began straightening up the living room, adjusted a picture on the wall, collected a few toys of Sparky's to take to the clinic in the morning when she went to visit him. Casting a critical eye around the room, she spied Gordon's letter under the table where it had somehow fallen.

She retrieved it, smoothed it out on her lap, read it through once more. Then she took it back to the bedroom, tucked it in the top drawer of her dresser.

Made in the USA
Lexington, KY
21 June 2015